Holly Starcross

● ● ●

Y

BERLIE DOHERTY

• • •

Holly Starcross

• • •

Greenwillow Books

An Imprint of HarperCollins*Publishers*

The text of this book is set in Bembo.

Library of Congress Cataloging-in-Publication Data

Doherty, Berlie.
Holly Starcross / by Berlie Doherty.
p.   cm.
"Greenwillow Books."
Summary: When fourteen-year-old Holly Starcross meets her
father for the first time in eight years, the experience changes the
way she thinks about him, her mother, and even herself.
ISBN 0-06-001341-9 (trade). ISBN 0-06-001342-7 (lib. binding)
[1. Divorce—Fiction. 2. Parent and child—Fiction. 3. England—Fiction.]
I. Title.
PZ7.D6947 Ho 2002   [Fic]—dc21   2001054808

1   2   3   4   5   6   7   8   9   10
First American Edition

For my dear friend
Johnny Yeoman

· 1 ·

My name? It's Holly Starcross.

"You don't know who I am," I said, and Mum raised her perfectly plucked eyebrows at me and carried on feeding Zoe from a plastic spoon. The twins giggled. I turned my back on them all and went up to my room, my sanctuary, where my posters of owls and leafy trees gave me windows, and my real window had soft green curtains like fields of grass. I felt upset. I felt ridiculous. I wish I hadn't said it. It just fell out, the way Lisa's tooth had fallen out that morning, tinged with blood and excitement.

Somewhere in the world outside there was a man following me.
Like a ghost, it walked with me, the image of that man in the street. But I wasn't afraid. Strangely, I was never afraid of that ghost.

I love my room. It is white, like a house of ice. It has a sky window that lets in the stars. I have a string of bells hanging by the other window, and when the wind stirs the curtains, they sing with tinkling chimes. Mum says I shouldn't leave the window open at night because it encourages Panto to use it as a cat flap. I don't mind, even when she flops across my face with her tummy wet from the dewy grass.

Panto belongs to my old life.

"If you really want to know who you are," came Lisa's voice from the other side of my door, "you're Holly."

"Prickly Holly," giggled Julian, who always agrees with everything she says.

"Prickly Holly Starcross," Lisa reminded him. "She's prickly *and cross.*"

They seemed to think this was hilarious. I could hear them giggling and wrestling on the landing. I ignored them. I switched on my computer and opened up my e-mail.

"Not Murray, like us, Prickly Holly Murray." Julian can't say Murray. *Muwwy*, it sounds like.

"Prickly Molly Hurry. Hickory Polly Mully." Lisa was ecstatic at the sound of her own wit.

I heard Mum come up the stairs and sweep them away from my door. The baby was crying now. Beautiful Zoe with her amethyst eyes. She's the best thing that's happened in my life for eight whole years.

Do you know who I am? I typed onto the screen. I addressed it to Zed—zed@brainwave.co.uk.

Mum came into my room. Zoe was squirming in her

arms. She put her down on the floor, and Zoe gazed up at me. Her cheeks were wet, and her eyes were huge and brimming with too much blue. I love Zoe. Everybody does. What a gift to be born with. You didn't have a wicked fairy at *your* christening, little beauty. I lifted her up, and she held out her arms and tugged at the chiming bells.

"I'd like to know what you think you mean by that," Mum said, nodding toward the message on the computer screen.

I pressed the mouse and flicked it away. "Nothing. If you don't know what it means, then it doesn't mean anything."

"And I'd like to know who this Zed person is."

I would, too. Zed is my guru, my planet, my deep sea, my best friend. My Einstein, my aboriginal. I *think* he's a he. He just appeared one day last autumn when I typed a simple question into the www.musicbox Web site. I go to Hazelwood School and I'm nearly fourteen. I probably shouldn't have put that, but our school is really well known for its music. And I don't play any musical instruments. I want to learn the cello, and Mum says I'm too old now. Is she right?

And I had written that because of what had happened earlier that day, when I was in our car with Mum and Henry and the twins. Zoe hadn't been born yet. We were all tired. I had my eyes closed; the twins were bickering. Henry put the car radio on, and suddenly I was inside my dream. I opened my eyes and found that the dream was still there. I was listening to my dream. Mum said, "Find something cheerful, for goodness' sake." But just as Henry was about to switch over, the music stopped and the announcer's voice said, "That was the Elgar Cello Concerto, played by Jacqueline du Pré."

"Mum, can I learn the cello?"

She didn't hear me, or chose not to hear me. Henry winked at me in the driving mirror. He does that when he senses trouble. It's his way of saying, "I'm on your side, but don't expect me to get on the wrong side of your mother by saying so." It's so easy, that is.

"I want to learn cello more than anything."

"It's out of the question," Mum said, cold as ice, in her no-arguing voice.

"Why?"

"I don't like them, that's why. I couldn't put up with all that scratching and scraping."

"Actually, it would be better to learn piano first," Henry said, trying to be helpful to both of us.

"And I can't be doing with one of those in the house either. It takes years to learn an instrument properly. You're probably too old by now. So forget it, Holly."

As I said, that was nearly a year ago, and it was where Zed came in.

The reply from him was: **When is a bird too old to sing?** Ghostly! I went straight to the music teacher at school and begged to have a go on the school cello. When I told him I couldn't have lessons, he raised his eyebrows. Of course he was surprised. It's not as though we couldn't afford it. There's no shortage of money in our house. "I just want to see if I can play it," I told him. So now he lets me loose in the music room, and sometimes he comes in and pretends to be doing some marking, and he shows me how to hold the bow and how the music should sound. And he says I'm a natural! Mum still doesn't know. Nobody knows except Sandy and Zed.

So, we've been e-mailing each other ever since. I think Zed's my best friend, but I never tell Sandy that. I like to imagine that Zed is Aaron Hamilton. Aaron the Fair One, Sandy and I call him. He plays double bass in the school orchestra. He's probably the best-looking boy in the universe.

Mum thinks Zed is my boyfriend. No, I don't tell her everything. I like to keep her guessing sometimes. After all, she does that to me. She stared at the monitor as the screen saver came on, flocks of colored birds swirling like rainbows. It's quite mesmerizing.

"Go to school," she said, shaking her head as if she were trying to pull herself out of a trance. "The twins are ready, and they're driving me mad. Get them out of the house."

Of course I have a third life: school.

Taking the twins to school was usually the nanny's job, but the last one left in a huff. They never stay long. I can't say I blame them. Mum is so demanding, and the twins are so high-spirited. Whenever a nanny leaves, which happens every few months, I have to take over. People think my mum is wonderful because she has a career in television and four children and she always looks like a movie star. She just smiles her beautiful smile and crosses her long legs and says all things are possible. It's true. They are. It's because I'm around.

It was one of those sharp, frosty mornings that I really

love. The twins tumbled out of the house behind me, biffing each other and giggling, happy as a pair of golden puppies, their cheeks as red as their gloves and their blue eyes sparkling. Everyone says how beautiful they are, and how pretty Zoe is. Don't imagine that I'm like them. I'm not. I'm the cuckoo in the nest, the alien from another planet.

When we arrived at their school gates, they raced into the yard without saying good-bye. They each have a little rucksack shaped like an animal clinging to their backs. Lisa has a monkey; Julian has a jaguar. I think their animals suit them, like totems. Zed once asked me what my totem is. **The ancients of Mexico threw ashes outside their door when a child was born. And whatever animal left its tracks in the ashes would be that child's totem for life,** he told me. I tried it. I put some flour outside the kitchen door that night. I'd only just gone up to my room when Panto jumped through my window, leaving floury footprints all over my duvet. I e-mailed Zed. **My totem is a cat.**

The symbol of liberty, Zed e-mailed back. **Try restraining a cat. Impossible! It means you will always go your own way. It's a good totem. Be good to your cat.**

Of course I will. Panto came with me from the other side.

I watched the twins running up to Miss Derby and hugging her. I thought about my first day at that school. There were no twins around in those days. I was six years old. I had just been torn away from my old life, my life with Daddy and Rosa and Nana and dusty-haired Grandpa Jake. I had no idea what had happened to me. I remember standing at the gates of the school holding Mum's hand. Mummy, she was then. And a tall blond man called Henry was holding her other hand. I'd met him only two days before that. I was supposed to call him Daddy.

They led me into the schoolyard and the children were billowing around me like those bright birds on my computer screen, only not silent like the birds but screaming and booing and chanting. I felt as if every sound they were making was tearing me into little pieces. I didn't cry when Mummy let go of my hand. I knew that she was going to leave me there. I let myself drop into deep darkness, where no one could touch me. Miss Derby's cold hand closed over mine. I wouldn't look at her. Pretend you're an alien, I told myself.

"Come and join your class," Miss Derby's high, strange voice said, from somewhere up in the air above me. Mummy had gone with the man with yellow hair. When I had to tell the class my name, I tried three times and nothing came out. "This little girl's voice has slid right down her tubes into her tummy," Miss Derby said. "Try once more, nice and loud."

"Holly Starcross," I said, nice and loud, and it was a good, bright, sure thing, like a familiar light in a black sky.

"Where d'you come from?" a boy called Mickey asked me later. "You don't talk like us."

"I come from Jupiter," I said, and deep down inside the dark well of myself, I started to cry.

But all that was nearly eight years ago. Now it was as if it had happened to somebody else. I left the twins and ran on toward my school. I always met Sandy at the corner. As soon as she saw me coming, she started to walk away from me, letting me know by the way her hair bounced on her shoulders that I was late. Her lovely new plum-colored shoes padded like cats' paws. How she had tormented her mother for those shoes!

When I caught up with her, I could see the ghost of her breath around her lips. "You look like a horse," I told her.

"So do you," she said. "Why the long face?"

"Very funny. Why the bony knees?" We started to run, hurling abuse at each other, laughing our heads off. If Aaron the Fair One had been anywhere around, we'd have stopped immediately.

"You don't know who I am," I said, and for some reason that just finished her off. She creased in half, chopping out that familiar staccato laugh of hers. Her father laughs in the same way.

"Go on then," I demanded. "Who am I?"

"Okay. You're . . . let's see: Miss Kenyan's pet; worst at games; half good at languages; Holly Murray in the register and Holly Starcross on your pencil case, that's weird that is; my best friend; you're soppy about Aaron the Fair One. . . . Will that do?"

Not quite. Is that really me? Is that all?

· 2 ·

That afternoon I came out of school on my own. I have to leave promptly to collect the twins. It was already growing a bit gloomy, and some of the cars had their headlights on. From time to time I could hear the crack of fireworks, even though it was still two weeks to fireworks night. It sounded like a war zone on the news, like rifle shots pitching off the buildings.

I used to love bonfire night when I was little. We made a great big wicker man to burn on the village field, and the fireworks exploded through his body in a shower of color and lights and shivered up to the black sky. That was in the old life. My father lifted me up onto his shoulders and said, "Look, Holly, those are your stars." He wasn't Dad; he was Daddy. His hair was fizzy against my cheek, and he had a deep laugh that rumbled around his chest when I snuggled my head against him. I could hear his heart beating, like a hidden drum.

I almost stepped in front of a car. It was moving so slowly that I thought it was stationary. The driver lifted his hand in apology and moved on, but just as slowly. I had the impression that he was staring at me. Even when he had gone past, I had the feeling that he was watching me in the mirror. And that I had seen him before. There is a man following me. No, I'd never told my mum. I didn't tell her everything. If I'd been with Sandy, I'd have pulled faces at him.

I ran across the road into the twins' school and had to drag them away from their computer game. Miss Derby said I was to tell my mother that she must make other arrangements for the twins because she wasn't prepared to look after them every night until I arrived. I could feel my face growing scarlet. I knew she was right and that she would already have asked Mum herself. I also knew that Mum would simply have wrinkled her forehead a little and then flashed the lovely smile that she wears on television and at parties, and she would have said that she would see what she could do. And then she would have forgotten about it, not because she had so many things on her mind but because she thought everyone should do as she wanted. And usually everyone did.

"I am not a child-minder, tell her," Miss Derby said.

"I will."

Julian ran ahead and started swinging on the gate. I called him back. A car was parked on the other side of the road, and even from that distance I had the strange, prickly feeling that someone inside it was watching me. I bent down, fussing a little about tying Lisa's shoelaces.

She tried to squirm away from me, doing silly little rabbit steps backward so I nearly toppled over.

"Come back, you nuisance." I laughed, feeling stupid because I thought I was being watched. But when I looked up, the car had gone. Julian was hanging upside down from the gates.

"That car's got a silly door," he said.

On the way home, we had to collect Zoe from the day nursery. She was dressed for leaving and was fast asleep in her pram, snugly wrapped in the fleecy outfit that her grandmother had made for her. Not *my* grandmother. Henry's mother. She is tall and angular, like a stork, and she peers at me in an astonished way as if she can't believe what she's seeing. She lives in France, in the huge house that we visit every summer. I don't think she likes children much, because when we arrive, she sighs and peers and pecks at us on both cheeks and then leaves us to do what we want. "So many children!" she says to Henry, waving her elegant, bony hands in the air as if she were drying her nail varnish. But she always gives us good presents.

Lisa wanted to push the pram, running ahead with it and veering it from side to side, making Zoe shriek. Julian was sulking, trailing so far behind that I had to keep stopping and going back for him. It was a nightmare, taking the twins home. It always is.

At the house, I gave the twins toast and jam and sat them in front of the television. I changed Zoe's nappy and sat cuddling her while I had my own tea; then I took her upstairs with me to my room. She sat on my bed, propped up on my pillow and gazing around at the world with her pellucid blue eyes. That's my favorite word at the moment. *Pellucid.* I collect words and try them out on Sandy and Zed. I put on some music, loud, wild, thumping music, and danced around the room, shaking my hair loose, watching myself in the mirror. Zoe chimed in with the music. I picked her up and swirled her around with me, and the beat got faster and wilder and we were both shrieking out loud. I didn't stop till Mum thudded on my door. "I've been in a baking hot studio all day. Have some consideration for others, please."

Zoe and I sank back onto my bed, exhausted. "As soon as I'm allowed to go to discos, I'm going to take you with me," I told her. "You're a funky babe." Downstairs, I could hear Lisa complaining that I hadn't let her have her favorite jam. I flipped on the computer and searched my e-mail. "Yes, funky babe! There's a message from Zed!" Best part of the day, my Zed messages. And there nearly always was one.

Do I know who you are? A good question. You may be a red giant or a white dwarf. You have it in you to be either, for you are made of the stuff of stars.

I giggled. Typical of Zed. I knew all about dwarfs and giants, too, so he needn't think he was baffling me with science. **Oh, thanks,** I typed back. **I don't want to know what I'm made of; I want to know who I am.**

I left the machine and lay on my bed next to Zoe. She twiddled with my hair. Her breath fluttered against my cheek. I tried to think what Zed meant. "What are you made of, Zoe?" I asked. She hiccuped and sighed deeply as if she were thinking about it. Blood and bone and tissue and nerves. And all the elements of the stars. But so is everybody, even Panto. "What makes you and me different from Panto, and what makes me different from you, eh?"

Zoe thought deeply and chuckled. Her fists grabbed air and held it tight.

I went back to the machine and typed. **Sometimes I think I'm a black dwarf. What if I don't really exist? What if I'm not really here at all?**

I felt a bit scared by that idea, and I wasn't quite sure if I meant it, but I could hear Mum coming back upstairs and calling for Zoe, and I sent the message quickly before she told me off about the phone bill. I was just closing the machine down when she came in. "Have you been mailing that boyfriend of yours again?" she asked.

I didn't say anything. He's not my boyfriend. Not Zed. Not unless he *is* Aaron Hamilton. But the sad truth is, I don't think Aaron Hamilton has even noticed me yet. And anyway, there's an awful lot of competition. It doesn't matter, though. It doesn't stop me loving him. I can't help it.

But who am I? I said my name out loud. Holly. Holly. Why was I named after a tree? Holly. How strange it sounded. But it was practically all I had left of my old life.

Before I went to school the next day, I sneaked into my e-mail again. **Remember that your black star is your planet and your constant companion. The force of its gravity spins you in orbit. Love the darkness of** your secret self. Love the brilliance of your visible self. Like yourself, Holly. I do.

Ghostly! *I do!* No, I didn't understand Zed's message, but that last bit was like a big juicy cherry on a cake. I thought about it all the way to school—all through the chatter of the twins, all through Julian's bleeding knee when he tripped over the next-door neighbor's bronchial spaniel, all through Sandy's interminable story about a video she'd watched with her mother the night before, and all through assembly, right up to the time when something Mr. Jessop said made my dreaming brain jump to attention.

"What did he say?" I mouthed at Sandy. I wanted to press a rewind button and run his talk back, but already people were shifting in their chairs, bags were being picked up, teachers were clapping their hands and ushering their classes out. I tugged Sandy's sweatshirt. "Prowler," she mouthed over her shoulder. "Watch out, Red Riding Hood."

"Alexandra Tiernan!" snapped Miss Duffy, sharp as a pistol. "Did I give you permission to speak?"

Prowler. I let that register and hang there in the middle of my daydream. It was something to think about later. It was something important.

There was a campaign of discipline at our school since the inspectors had been and had given the place a bad report. Cheerful, absentminded Mrs. Bealy had gone, and with her all the dawdling, gossiping strolls from one classroom to another between lessons. Instead we had Mr. Jessop and his regime of silence in corridors, files to the right, files to the left, queuing for meals, standing up, and opening doors for teachers. It was like a game at first, though the novelty soon wore off. But Mr. Jessop couldn't stop me daydreaming, could he? He couldn't peer through my eyes and spy on what was going on inside my head. *The darkness of my secret self.* Nothing in there usually.

So Sandy closed her mouth and rolled her eyes and went on her way to the science block, and I completely forgot to ask her again. But there was a nagging in my head, like the ruffle the wind makes on water. Something had become disconnected. I was disjointed. I was being pulled in several directions. Later, now, I can look back and see that everything belonged: the black dwarf, the cello, the battered car, and even, though goodness knows how it got there, the wren.

The wren happened much later that evening. The sound of the cello was still singing in my head, because I had had a lesson from the music teacher that day. He came into the music room when I was practicing and stood listening for a bit, and then he sat down with his own cello and gave me a proper lesson. My hands were sweating in case I played too many wrong notes and showed myself up. I can't explain why the cello is so important to me. It's something to do with my dreams, because in my dreams, many times, I hear music being played, and it fills me with such a sense of longing that when I wake up again, I hardly know what to do with myself or where I am. I didn't know till much later that it was a cello I was hearing.

In my dream there is a fire burning and the room is dark with its shadows and soft with its lights. There are low voices talking. And in my dream someone lifts me and carries me up winding stairs, and I can feel the soft rub of wool against my cheek, and all the time I can hear the deep, thrilling sound of music. I would try to will this dream to come by placing myself in the firelit room. I would name the objects in a kind of chant in my head, as if it were a magical incantation that would summon up the music. And sometimes it did. The firelight, the heavy oak mantel, the long creamy curtains, the chair with the fringe of tassels: Those are the things that would make my music come.

· 3 ·

Anyway, the wren. Panto was in the back garden, prowling through the grass. I sat on the kitchen windowsill watching every furtive, measured movement. At the same time, my brain was clicking back to that morning: assembly, Mr. Jessop, prowler. "There is concern that there is a prowler in the neighborhood." I thought of the battered car with the painted door that didn't match. I thought of the face, watching me. The slow passage of the car as I knelt to tie Lisa's laces. I went cold, inside and out.

Panto gathered herself together and pounced. She turned, and I could see she had a bird in her mouth.

"Panto!" I banged on the window. "Drop it!" I ran to the door and opened it, and she charged in with the bird still clamped in her mouth. I grabbed for her tail, and she skittered around the room, leaping out of my grasp onto the windowsill. The plant pot shattered on the floor, scattering shards of pot and soil and blood-red geranium petals. The bird fluttered free, crazy with fright. I threw Panto into the lounge, where she yowled with rage, waking up Zoe.

"What on earth's going on?" Mum demanded, half asleep herself in front of the television. She came into the kitchen.

"Close the door," I shouted. "Don't let Panto in."

The bird was flinging itself against the window. It shimmered around the room, beating against the walls, then back to the window and around the kitchen again.

"Let that thing out," Mum shouted, ducking.

It had landed on the pan shelf. I climbed onto a stool and managed to cup the bird in my hands. I could feel the pitiful beat of the bird's small heart. It was a wren. Such a tiny, warm, helpless, throbbing thing. How it trusted me, its eyes blinking, its beak wide open.

"Poor little thing, I've got you safe, I've got you safe," I told it.

Julian ran in. "Let me see, let me hold it."

"Just stroke it," I said. "Very gently now. It's very frightened."

He stood on tiptoe, his tongue between his lips, holding his breath with concentration. "It's warm," he whispered. "It's nice."

"We'll let him go now."

I went outside, holding the wren snugly inside my hand. I didn't want to part with it, such a little, fragile, trusting creature. Its tiny claws grasped my finger. I sat on the edge of the raised patio where Henry cooks bar-becues in the summer and opened my hands. It stayed still, watching me more confidently now, head cocked to one side to look up at me. "You've got to take your chance now, little thing." I knelt, held my hands underneath a low bush, and tipped the bird out onto the soil. It could shelter there, look at the world and make sense of it, decide if it still belonged. Julian banged on the kitchen window, holding a squirming Panto in his arms. "Panto wants her tea," he mouthed. I shook my head at him and walked around the garden for a bit—Henry's tidy lawn, bare soil border, and neatly pruned roses— then sat by the patio again. I bent down and looked under the bush.

I can't explain why I suddenly felt so sad. I heard Julian shout, "Holly's crying." Mum came out and sat next to me. She put her arm around me.

"I'm not," I said.

"Is it dead?"

"It's gone."

"Do you know, Holly, I wish I could make sense of you." She paused for a minute, as if she was waiting for me to say something to help her. I couldn't think of anything. "Okay, Miss Moodiwarp. Come on in and eat."

She went back inside, leaving the kitchen door open. Henry had come home. I could hear the twins crowing around him, Mum chattering to him as she laid the table. I was forgotten. It was peaceful out there. It was turning to dusk, and the first stars were coming out. I lay on my back and looked at them, trying to remember the names of the shapes they made. They looked enormous that night. The sky was a great black orb with stars pricking holes of light into it. And the earth was spinning, spinning. I pressed my back into the cold ground, spreading out my arms, holding on. One false move and I would be flung away from the surface of the earth and spiraled into space. I closed my eyes against the dizzy stars. Dwarfs and giants. A tiny wren that made me cry. Cello. Patterns spinning around the sky.

"By the way," I said to Mum when I went back into the house, "I can't collect Lisa and Julian anymore."

"Is that so?"

"It's not me. It's Miss Derby. She says to remind you that she's not a child-minder."

"She said *what*?"

"And you'll have to make arrangements to have them collected earlier. You *have* to, Mum. She's always telling you."

Mum was buttering bread. She swept her hair away from her eyes with the back of her hand, her face tilted up to the light.

"Tell her Henry and I have got two more weeks in the studio, that's all. We'll have a new nanny long before then. She knows that anyway. Why does she have to be so difficult? It's you, isn't it, dawdling out of school?"

I felt like shaking her. "You can tell her yourself," I said. I helped myself to a piece of bread from the plate and smeared it with Marmite. I walked around the kitchen, eating it.

"I'll take care of it," Henry said. Henry the Peacemaker, Henry the hero. I ought to like him, really. He kissed Mum, taking the knife out of her hand as if it were a weapon that she was threatening me with.

"Don't you worry your pretty head about it any longer."

"Yuk." I took two apples from the fruit bowl and juggled them.

"I've got an office temp who's dying of boredom. It'll give her a break to leave the office at three, pick the twins up, and take them to Zoe's minder. Then they can stay there till Holly picks them all up."

I dropped the apples. "You're a wizard, Henry," I said as scornfully as I could.

He took it as a compliment. "It's no trouble."

"You just have to wave your wand, and all her dreams come true. *And* you're a handsome prince. Isn't she lucky!" I waltzed around Mum, waving an imaginary wand, and then danced out. It felt good. It made my anger swirl away to nothing. It made the twins laugh, too.

Later I was on the landing upstairs, and I overheard Mum telling Henry that she was sick of my funny moods. "All teenagers have funny moods," he told her. "She'll grow out of them."

He should know, I suppose. He has three of his own, in France. Twice a year he flies out to spend a week or so with them. Mum hates it when he goes, but she never wants to go with him. They never come here. He calls them his three rascals. I'm sure he misses them a lot.

And whenever he mentions them, I ache to know about my father. Daddy, locked in a time capsule somewhere out in space where my old life used to be. I can't remember his face. I can't remember his voice. It doesn't mean I've forgotten him. The last time I saw him he was driving over to visit Vincent's farm about two hours away. I wanted to go with him. I loved going to Vincent's. While they were talking about horses, I used to play with the children there, sliding down the hay in the barns, swinging on a rope that hung from a great chestnut tree, over the stream and back again, over and back, shrieking and daring one another to jump off into the water. When I did, my father would roll me up in his jacket and let me lie across the backseat of the car, pretending I was a big salmon that he'd fished up for tea. But that day, that last day, Mum wouldn't let me go with him. I ran alongside the car, waving good-bye till we got to the cattle grid. The car bounced over it, fast, rattling the bars. My father was laughing and waving back to me. After that I never saw him again.

"See if you can talk her out of it," Mum said to Henry. "You're better with her than I am." Which was true. We're always arguing, Mum and I. "And try to get her off that wretched computer. I'm sorry we ever bought it for her."

I went back into my room and shut the door. I wanted to e-mail something to Zed, but I wasn't sure what to say now. I was a bit knocked back by that last message. **Like yourself, Holly. I do.** *Did* he know me? What if, just what if, it was Aaron Hamilton? After all, it had to be a musician. What if it *was* Aaron Hamilton who had answered my question in the Internet music club? Would he recognize my name? Probably not. But I had said which school I went to. What if he watched me every time I went to practice, secretly knowing it was me? Perhaps he was too shy to speak to me in person. (I could imagine Sandy snickering: "Aaron Hamilton! *Shy!*") But he might have fallen in love with me, and the only way he could talk to me was through the Net. It was a wonderful daydream, and I gave myself up to it completely.

Henry knocked on my door with his foot. "Holly, I've brought you some coffee." His eyebrows questioned me. Was it all right to come in? I supposed it was, so I shrugged. He glanced at the screen as he placed the mug on my table. "Homework?" he asked casually, pleasantly.

I shrugged again. He could see it wasn't.

"Maybe it's time you got down to it."

"I've only got French."

"Would you like me to hear some vocab?"

He said it in a mock French accent, and I smiled dutifully. He really was trying very hard. I closed down the computer, and the room seemed to sigh with the silence. I swiveled around to look at him. He pretended he was twiddling an imaginary mustache. I could hear Mum bathing Julian and Lisa. Zoe was in the bathroom with them, gurgling in her chair. She would want to be in the bath, but Julian would splash her and make her cry, just as I used to do with them.

I couldn't bear it when anyone made Zoe cry. Sometimes, when I took her out for walks, I would push her through the park, running with the pram to make her laugh, rocking her under the splashes of sunlight coming through the trees, talking to her all the time. I hoped people would think she was mine. "What a good little mother," I imagined them saying. "But she can't be more than thirteen or fourteen."

Actually, there are girls of my age who have babies,

even in England, really and truly. I think it would be awful. There's another side to having babies that they can't have known about, or they'd never have let it happen. Even Zoe isn't always pretty and cooing and smelling of talc and sleep. Sometimes she's red-faced and screaming, stinking of nappies and sick, and she doesn't know the difference between night and day. I don't think I'm ever going to have babies.

I took my French book out of my bag and started to do the homework exercise. Henry sat watching me for a bit. Maybe he wanted to talk or maybe he just wanted to get out of having to bathe the little ones. I ignored him anyway. After a bit he went out, leaving the door open. The twins were bouncing on their beds. I could hear Henry romping around the room with them, pretending to be a big bad wolf, making them squeal, and then he rolled them into their beds and started to tell them a story. I'd have given anything to have been able to go into their room and sit on one of the beds, cuddling Zoe maybe, listening to the story with them. But I couldn't. To tell you the truth, I didn't know how to do it.

· 4 ·

I was eating sandwiches in the school canteen next day, and Helena Griffiths said, "Did that man find you?"

"What man?" I could feel myself blushing. I thought of Zed. I thought of Aaron Hamilton.

"Some man outside school last night. He said he was looking for Holly Starcross."

My heart did a slow cartwheel. "Looking for me?"

"The prowler!" Sandy said dramatically.

Rachel Harland put her hand to her mouth. "Oh, flippers, I never thought of that."

"He asked us what you looked like." Helena went on peeling her orange unconcernedly. She must have heard the thumping of my heart. "I told him you were just about the ugliest girl in school and that he'd be able to smell you a mile off. Swap half my orange for half your banana?"

"Was there really someone?" Sandy asked. "We ought to tell Mr. Jessop if there was."

"You're making it up," I said. "And you can keep your rotten orange."

Helena broke a piece of orange peel and put it under her lips, as if she had orange teeth. She smiled around at us.

"More to the point, can we remember what he looked like," Rachel said, "if there had to be an identity parade?"

"Shut up," I said. "You're being stupid, both of you."

Helena peeled her orange teeth away and wiped her mouth. She stood up to go. "Easy. Middle-aged. Middle height. Nose, eyes, mouth, the usual sort of thing."

She went to the bin and dropped the peel into it. We stood up to follow her.

"I'd remember his car, though," Rachel said. "A right old banger."

There went my heart again. "Did it have an orange door?"

"Oh, you know him! I was beginning to get a bit worried. I thought you were about to get kidnapped." Rachel ran off after Helena.

Sandy squeezed my arm. "See you!"

I stared after them, then turned away. No, I didn't know him. But I remembered catching his eyes in the driving mirror. I remembered knowing he was watching me when I was in the schoolyard tying Lisa's laces. And I remembered how I had felt then. It wasn't fear. It was a strange, spacey, dislocating sensation as if part of me were lifting up and flying off on its own, a feeling of something beyond myself taking control. I had never experienced it before, not in real life. It belonged to my dreams. Yet it wasn't fear. I tried to put it out of my mind.

As I was going toward the gates at the end of the

afternoon, Maria Cartwright from my French group broke away from a bunch of gossips and clopped over to me like a carthorse in her heavy shoes. She was breathless and bossy and important with news.

"Go out the other gate," she said. "There's a man waiting for you."

I tried to laugh it off. I was quite excited by all this attention.

"He's just asked me if Holly Starcross is in school today, and when I said I didn't know for certain, he asked me what you look like. He's weird."

"Weird?"

"He must be."

The other girls began to saunter toward me. They had a kind of knowing awe in their faces.

"Go to Mr. Jessop," Maria insisted. "Now. He'll get someone to take you home."

They all gathered around me in a protective group. I felt stifled by them. Sandy joined them and put her arm around me. Maria's eyes were nearly swallowing her face.

"I'm all right," I insisted. I'd had enough attention. I wanted to go away and think.

"Shall we walk home with you?" Sandy suggested. "We should be quite safe if there's six of us."

"But what about me?" Rachel Harland moaned. "I live in the opposite direction. If we all walk one another home, I'm bound to be last."

"I tell you, I'm going to be all right. I'll get the bus. I don't have to get Lisa and Julian tonight, anymore, ever!" I tried to laugh brightly. I ran off, leaving them behind. I had no intention of catching the bus. It didn't go anywhere near my house. But I didn't want an escort of angels of doom, screaming and giggling at every car that went past.

The roads were busy. No one was going to snatch me off the pavement. Even so, I hugged the side that was nearest to the shops. I looked in the windows at the reflections of all the passing cars. I was very clever. I didn't take my usual route, past the infants and junior school, across the park. I took the long way around. For once in my life I wished I were like Sandy and Rachel and had my own mobile phone. Then I would know I would be 100 percent safe. But who would I phone? Mum would be in the middle of a shoot. When Henry was producing a program, he was always too desperately important to interrupt. I imagined his temp answering his phone. She would have flossy yellow hair—everyone around Henry has yellow hair—and she would be painting her nails coral pink out of boredom, and she would sigh when the phone rang because her nails would still be wet. She would waft her fingers about and pick up the handset with the tips of her thumb and second finger, and she would coo breathily into the mouthpiece. But no—I was forgetting—even now her painted nails would be encircling the steering wheel of her specially hired car, and she would be mincing her way through the traffic with Lisa and Julian tucked up in the backseat. I hoped she made them use the seat belts. Anyway, that ruled out Coral Nails. It left no one. If I had Zed's phone number, I would ask him what to do.

I went into a newspaper shop and stood flicking through magazines. I can't be bothered with them, really. I like books better. I just wanted to look at the pictures. I just wanted to think. Dear Zed. Why aren't I being sensible? Why didn't I go to Mr. Jessop and tell him what Maria had told me? And I knew the answer. I actually wanted to see the man in the car again. But I didn't dare say why.

I bought a magazine and came out of the shop, stuffing it into my schoolbag. I dropped my change as I tried to put it into my purse. The car was there.

It was heading away from me. The driver couldn't have seen me. I could have run back into the shop and stayed there for a few more minutes. I was in a slow-motion film, yet everything around me was speeding—the traffic, the people on the pavement, the shadows and lights in the windows—while I was moving as slow as dreams. I stepped down a side alley. I'd never been into it before. I looked around it with slow wonder, like a little child. When I reached the end, I found it was blocked off. It was intended just for delivery vans. A boy was whistling a high, sweet tune as he trundled a pile of cardboard boxes out to the garbage. I turned around and began to walk back. I felt as if I were drifting in a dream, yet I could hear the echo of my footsteps and the flap of my bag like a broken wing against my side. And there was the car.

The driver was getting out. I saw his face at last, a kind, smiling, questioning face. He was middle-aged, a bit stocky. He had black, curly hair that was going gray. I wanted to think. I wanted to think. I put one foot in front of the other, again, again, and walked without any sense of where I was, through the doorway of Sainsbury's. The automatic glass doors closed soundlessly behind me. I wanted to think. "Holly?" I heard him call. "It is Holly, isn't it?" I wanted to think. But I knew the voice. From my other life I knew the voice.

Instead of turning around, I went and hid among the cereal packets. I was frightened in case the man was a prowler after all, a stranger who knew my name, haunting me to snatch me away from my life. I wanted him to go away. I wanted to see him again. I put down the packet of chocolate-flavored crispies at last and went out of the shop. The man had gone. The car had gone.

That night when I went to my room, I pulled open the blind that covered my roof window. I had a skylight to the stars. If I stood on the bed and pushed it open, I could see the city, lying in a jewel bed of amber lights. I imagined the stranger who knew my name circling the city boundaries, coming closer, circling my road, padding around the shady gardens of my house. I thought of a hungry wolf coming down from the mountains with a scent in his snout and a taste on his tongue. For a moment that seemed to last forever, the clouds pressed down onto the city horizons and became mountains shrouded in flimsy mist, and the jewel eyes of the night city became animal eyes staring out of the darkness, and the swish of tires on the road was like the ceaseless tread of the wolf-stranger, cunning and resolute and single-minded, searching for me. I was afraid, and yet I was not afraid. The stranger was walking out of my past, and I had a cunning of my own that was just as strong as his. The cunning was to know his story.

· 5 ·

How do you hold the print of the sound of a voice in your mind, or the sense of a face, a smile, a way of walking? How do you hold a sense of love?

I loved my dad.

I should have gone with him to Vincent's farm that last day of my old life. Everything might have been different if I had. It was raining. My mother said, "You can't go. It will be too wet to play outside with Vincent's children." I had cried. She stroked my hair. "Stay with me and we'll . . ." I don't know what. I don't remember. I kept on crying.

I remember that she was strange all day after my father went. She was tense and troubled one minute and laughing out loud the next; she was busy in her room, and she was listless, sitting on the bed, staring out at the hills that were robbed of their color by the mist. When it was time for me to go to bed, she said, "Don't go to bed, stay up with me." But I wanted to sleep. Her strange mood upset me. I wanted to go to bed and wait there for Daddy to come home and tell me a story. "Daddy won't be home till late," she told me. "Stay up and sit with me." At last she let me go to bed. I slept, and then she woke me up and carried me out of the room. Her face was bright, and her breath came fast and painful. She put my coat on over my pajamas. They were my favorite pajamas. They had teddy bears scattered across them, dancing, holding the strings of yellow balloons, red balloons, blue balloons. She put my shoes and socks on, and her hands were shaking. I knew something important was happening, so important that I was frightened to ask her what it was.

I followed her down the stairs, and there was a tall blond-haired man standing by the door. He was combing his hair in the mirror, bending his knees a little. He was surrounded by carrier bags and suitcases. He turned around, crouched down to me, and cupped my chin. I shrank away from him. There was a strange, sharp scent on his face.

"So this is little Holly."

"Holly, say hello to Henry," my mother said. "He's going to take us to his house."

She glanced quickly at him and away again. She bent down, and her hair swung across her face, hiding her eyes from me. Henry stood up.

"Right. I'll carry the stuff to the car." He propped open the door with the black foot iron and ran outside. I could see the rain slanting across the light, gleaming streaks of silver.

"Where's Daddy? What about Daddy?"

"He's not coming," my mother said. "We're not going to live with Daddy anymore."

I looked at the rain. I looked through the rain at the tall blond man stooping into the white car.

"It'll be better," my mother said.

I started to cry. "I want Daddy."

And my mother said, "Well, I don't. It will be better with Henry."

I ran away from her into the living room. It was dark except for the pale light from the dead embers of the fire in the hearth. I could hear Henry coming in for more bags, stamping his feet on the doormat that was like the bristles of a brush.

"She'll be all right," I heard my mother say.

I sat in the dark with my face buried into the embroidered cushion on the settee. I could hear them both running backward and forward to the car. I could hear the rain splashing from the roof. I heard the car door slam. I thought they were going to go without me, and I kept very still in the dark. I thought they were going to leave me alone in the big ticking house until Daddy came back from seeing Vincent about the horses.

Then my mother came into the room and put her arms around me. I could smell her hair and the rain and the scent she wore on her dark green coat. "It's lovely in Henry's house. He's got a television. He's got all sorts of lovely things."

"I want Daddy." The kittens sprawled out of their box by the fire. "I can't come. I've got to look after the kittens."

The blond man stood in the doorway, rubbing his hands together. "Right?"

"Come on," my mother said. "Now." Her voice was firm, and it frightened me a little. She began to pull me away from the cushion, and I bent down and snatched up one of the kittens. It wriggled for freedom, but I clutched it to me in the same way that my mother was clutching me. When we got to the door, she lifted me in front of her and ran me out to the car. I don't think she knew that I had the kitten with me.

Henry swung the car around so quickly that mud spattered up against the windows. Mum leaned back in her seat. "Thank God," she said. "Thank God. I'll never have to look at this place again."

I looked back at the cottage, through the silvery rain dancing in the car headlights.

"Do we need to shut those gates?" I heard the blond man say, and I heard the high, nervous tinkling of my mother's laughter.

"Forget the gates. I'm never going to have to bother about those gates again."

And that was when I knew for certain that I was leaving my old life behind forever.

· 6 ·

That night, the night I ran into Sainsbury's and hid among the cereal packets, the night I opened my sky window and watched the star wolf prowling, that night I thought about my old life as I had never allowed myself to think about it before. I remembered a dark stable. It is lit by the dim orange light of an oil lamp. The straw is gleaming like Rumpelstiltskin's gold. I am a little girl in my daddy's arms. Maybe I am two years old. Betty shuffles her hooves, breathing heavily. I am a little bit afraid of her, and I put my arms around my daddy's neck. I can smell his sweat, like the tomatoes that grow in the porch. I hide my face in his hair, half playing fear. "Look," he whispers. "Look, little Holly Starshine. Look in the straw." I turn my head, still playing fear. He bends down and brings me close to Betty's withers, and now I can see that the dark, still shape at her hooves is not her shadow but a foal. It is just born. It gleams like a floating moon. As I watch, it turns its head around, and its eyes, which are shining in the light, watch me. They seem to know me. My breath is caught in my throat. The foal struggles to her feet. I am crowing; that was what I remembered, my own voice crowing into the holy stillness of the barn.

My daddy hushes me. "What shall we call her?"

"Rosa." My voice is tiny with awe now.

"She's for Holly," he whispers. "You'll grow up together."

And another thing I remembered was this: It is from my new life, and it is the sudden knowing that my mother has grown round and heavy. She is too big to take me on her knee. She says I am too big. She tells me that soon I will have two babies to play with. And when they come, they are tiny, red, wrinkled, roaring things, and my mother is totally absorbed with them.

And these babies go on forever. They don't go away. I wish them to, but my wish is never answered. One day I am sitting on the edge of my bed. The screaming twins are asleep, and I have my mother to myself. She is brushing my hair, which is always wild, not sleek and golden like hers.

I say something then that I haven't been able to say since the day she and Henry snatched me away from my old life. "I want Daddy."

She puts down the brush and loops her arms around me and holds my head against her softness. "Darling, darling Holly." Like a bedtime song, like a kiss. "Henry is your daddy now."

In the drawer underneath my bed there is a shoe box.

It once held a pair of patent leather shoes with buckled straps. Grandmother Murray bought them for my first Christmas in my new life. And since then the box has held a secret. It is a pile of letters.

"DERE Daddy. Plees com and tek me home."

"Dere daddy I want to see Rosa."

"Dere daddy were are you and were is Rosa?"

Drawings of a horse with a huge, long head, and a mane like black swinging hair, and knees that bend the wrong way on legs like sticks. Nobody knew about the letters. They never got posted because I didn't know where I was from. It was a cottage next to a farm. It was in a valley that had hills like green sleeping horses. It had a huge whispering tree outside my window.

My mother stops brushing my hair and tries to tame it into bunches. She picks two green rubber bands out of the dish by my bed. They should have been blue ones. I am wearing my blue dress, and she is always so careful about matching my dress, my socks, my bands.

"You *must* try calling him Dad. He wants that."

"I want my real daddy."

My mother turns my head around with a sharp, hurting movement. In the mirror I can see my white face, with her hand cupping my chin, and behind her I can see through the doorway to where Henry is standing, jigging the twins in his arms.

"Holly, try to understand. Your daddy made me very unhappy. I couldn't live there anymore. All those animals. All that mess. All that mud in the yard. Don't you remember it?"

I nod. My mother is talking to me like a grown-up,

watching me in the mirror as she speaks, watching herself, watching Henry.

"It was all right for him. He was used to it. I made a mistake. Do you understand? I thought I would like it there, but I hated it. Henry makes me happy. I'm happy here with Henry and you and the babies. You want me to be happy, don't you?"

I fling my arms around her and cling to her, tight, tight, never wanting to let go. But the hurt inside me is so deep that I don't know where it begins or where it ends. That was the only thing she ever said about my father: that he made her unhappy.

And that was why I never told her about the letters I had written or asked her where I could send them. I was afraid. She had left my daddy because he made her unhappy. What if she left me, too?

· 7 ·

Do you know about the man in the ice?

I laughed out loud when I saw Zed's latest e-mail. The man in the ice! Zed, you are so full of mystery and knowledge. You get hold of me and fling me out of myself. I typed back simply **No. Tell me.**

The answer came straightaway. Somewhere in the world, across the floating particles of space, Zed was speaking to me, touching my thoughts, hearing them and knowing them. Who are you, Zed? That was the question I'd never asked. Almost, I didn't want to know.

Two people walking in the Austrian Alps found a body in the ice. His head and shoulders were sticking out. The ice was melting away from him in the sun. Scientists dug him out. Guess how long he had been there?

Hmm, Zed. I needed to think about this for a bit. Surely the Alps aren't that remote, even though they're

so high. People are always walking there, climbing, ski-
ing. A group from school went there last winter (includ-
ing, I thought with a knowing smirk, Aaron Hamilton).
People got lost down crevasses, covered in avalanches.
Perhaps . . . **Five years.**

"Holly!" Mum called from downstairs. "Are you
interested in eating anything tonight?"

No. I wasn't. I didn't want food. I wanted answers.

"Will you answer me, please, Holly?"

"No," I shouted back. "Thanks."

The downstairs door closed. The television clamor
receded. Then on a strange impulse I added, **What
about the man in the battered car? Do you know
about him?**

Another message. **I'm talking about a man who
was perfectly preserved. Not a skeleton. His skin
still there, tough as leather. His shoes. Bits of
clothing.**

So. Someone who'd been preserved for many years.
Zed wouldn't be so interested if it were a recent death.
Maybe it was a shepherd, alone up there with the sky
and the stars and his wandering flock. Falling and hurting himself. Lost up there with only the knowing stars
to see. Five hundred years? I tried to imagine that.
Could it be possible?

**Holly Starcross, this is a marvelous thing. Think
about it. Don't let it slip away from you. Hold it in
your head and wonder at it. He was five thousand
years old.**

I closed down the computer and lay on my bed in
the dark. I pulled my duvet around me to keep warm.

The sky window was still open. I must have drifted into a dream. I must have been lifted out into the stars and floated there, looking down at the pale, dark-haired girl lying in a snowy swirl of white. I am the ice person. Little by little people are digging me out, as a carving emerges out of wood or stone. They are not scientists who are bringing me out, but old, strange people with long silvery hair and dextrous, caring hands. They know what to do. At last they lift me out of the ice, and I hold up my hands to a blazing sun and shout with all my strength, "Who am I? Where am I?" And these kind people with hair shivering like mist around their shriveled faces look at one another with puzzled frowns because my language is alien to them.

Panto scratched at my door. I cuddled her and carried her downstairs to the living room. They were all watching a family game show on television. Julian was in his pajamas, curled up on Henry's knee, his face round and pink with laughing at the inane antics of some poor victim on the screen who was being doused with purple slush. Lisa was laughing so much that she was hiccuping at the same time. She was sitting on the floor, leaning on the sofa between Henry and Mum. Zoe in her creamy sleep suit half asleep in Mum's arms. At the side of the settee there was a pile of plates with pizza crusts heaped on the top one like a mound of abandoned false teeth. A couple of beer cans, a Coke can, a half-finished cup of black coffee. In the flickering television light they all looked so golden. Pale yellow shining hair, all of them, though Mum's is dyed. Honey gold skin. A golden, sunny, happy family. I went and stood in front of the television screen and spoiled it for them. There were cries of protest from all of them, even Zoe.

"Your pizza's in the oven," Mum said. "Dry as a bone by now."

"Have you got any old photographs?" I asked.

"Move, Holly. You make a better door than a window."

"Family photographs. Me when I was little."

"The drawer under the music center. You know very well."

Of course I knew. "And my dad."

"For goodness' sake, Holly."

"I want to see a photograph of my father."

"She's probably doing a school project," Henry said across Julian's head. Reasonable, always reasonable.

"This has got nothing to do with school projects." Mum propped Zoe against a cushion, jumped up, and pulled me away from the television. She marched me into the kitchen. Her fingers on my arm hurt me. I was glad they hurt. It made me gasp. It made me slap her hand away.

She slammed the door shut behind her. "Never let me hear you say that in front of Henry. He's brought you up for the last eight years. He's your father. You know that."

I shook my head. Mum sighed and folded her arms, rocking backward and forward, staring at me, shaking her head. Her eyes were glassy with anger or tears, I couldn't tell which. Both, if she felt the way I felt. She turned away from me and opened the oven door. It sticks, and she has to tug it, nearly losing her balance every time. It was something that Henry kept promising to fix. She brought out a dried-up pizza and tipped it onto a plate from under the grill. The plate was hot, and she slid it quickly onto the work surface. "You've ruined this. Gawking at that computer. I'm sorry we ever bought the thing."

"Have we?" I insisted.

"Have we what?" She was making a cup of coffee, rattling the spoon inside a near-empty jar of Nescafé. I wanted to take the jar off her and throw it through the window, shattering ice.

"Photos."

"Look." She banged mugs onto the metal tray. It had ginger cats and yellow roses painted on it; I bought it her for Christmas when I was ten. "Understand this. When you walk away from your husband, you do not bring his photograph with you. I never wanted to see him again when I left that house, and thank God, I never will. Eat your pizza. Please eat your pizza."

As if it mattered. To please her, I cut a corner off the pizza slice. I toyed with it, chasing it around the plate the way Panto chases an inert scrap of paper. "I can't remember what he looked like." My voice was stretched like a string of chewing gum. I couldn't help it. I pushed the plate away. Hear me, Mum. Understand my language.

She was about to open the door, the tray of steaming mugs and chocolate biscuits balanced on the palm of one hand. "You don't need a photograph. I'm sorry to say he looked just like you. You can't help it, but you're the image of your father." She said it as if it were a joke. "Every time I look at you, I see him." She opened the lounge door. The room burst into the hysterical laughter of the television game show, then closed away again. I tipped the pizza into the bin.

Next day at school all the talk was of the prowler. He had been seen by several girls in my year, who all reported that he drove a battered car with an odd door. All the girls thought he had been following them. Amelia Smith. Melissa Hendry. Caroline Court. I don't think we looked much like one another, except for one thing. Amelia was the tallest by far, and Melissa was twice my weight. Caroline wore glasses. But Sandy pointed out that we all had dark, curly hair. Even then, we were different. Mine was longer and messier. The other three had short curls cropped as tight as rosebuds, the way Mum wanted me to have mine.

One other girl said she'd seen him, and that was Auriole Cooper. She had a dramatic tale of being chased through the park by him. "He nearly caught me." She had a captive audience in the girls' cloakroom. She was combing her hair in the mirror, long, sleek, foxy red. "He put his hand on my shoulder and pulled me round toward him. I screamed and kicked out at his doodahs, and he staggered back and fled." She gazed into her own green eyes. "He won't be able to do you know what for a long time, girls."

I let her boastful laughter float away from me. Nobody ever believed a word she said. I looked around the cloakroom at the other faces. Amelia, Melissa, and Caroline. All had dark, curly hair. Like mine. Like mine. I slid away from them. I said nothing. I kept to myself the fact that the man had called out my name. Even when we were called into the school hall by the Head of Year and told that the police had been informed and were patroling the neighborhood, that we were to be escorted to the buses, and that we were on no account to speak to any stranger on our way home, I said nothing. Rumors were flying; hysteria ran like shivers of lightning around the school; screams of laughter erupted in nervous flares. I kept my mouth shut. I stared out the window, and I kept my mouth shut.

The truth was, I wanted to see him again.

There were no sightings of him for the rest of the week. Auriole claimed that a bunch of blood red roses had been left on her doorstep. By the time Friday came, everyone had stopped talking about him. There were new things to talk about: Halloween parties, half term, fireworks night. I helped Mum make a witch outfit for Lisa and a wizard's cloak for Julian. We cut stars and moons out of a white sheet and sewed them onto their cloaks. Mum bought a pumpkin and hollowed it out, and I cut eyes and a mouth and put a candle inside it. Mum made the pulp into soup, and we ate it in the dark with just the pumpkin candle lighting the table, and Henry told us a ghost story. The candlelight flickered around all their golden faces, and I held Zoe warm and rapt, her breath catching in soft little trembles as she struggled to keep awake. When Henry took the little ones up to bed, Mum said, "Let's have a cup of hot chocolate. Just you and me." We sat in the quiet room in the pumpkin light.

"I remember a Halloween party," Mum said, "when I was about ten. The girls next door invited me to their house. They asked me if I wanted to fly like a witch, and I said no, but they sat me in a chair and tied me in it and put a blindfold around my eyes, and I flew. I really flew. They told me I was definitely a witch but I mustn't tell anyone. I was so frightened that I had nightmares all week. But I never told a soul that I was a witch. Till now." She laughed, and I laughed with her.

"I suppose that makes me a bit of a witch, too. And Lisa and Zoe. Imagine Zoe on a broomstick!"

"What are you two laughing at?" Henry asked from the doorway.

"Oh, nothing. Secrets," Mum said.

"Ah. Girl talk."

Henry walked through into the kitchen. Panto flopped off the settee and followed him, asking for food in her best voice.

"I'd completely forgotten about it till tonight," Mum said, "when Henry was telling us that witch story. But I've just realized how they did it. Hang on."

She led me into the kitchen and sat me on one of the straight chairs, then fastened me into it with tea towels. I couldn't stop giggling.

"What's going on?" Henry asked.

"Just seeing if Holly's a witch."

Panto mewed. I could feel her rubbing against my ankle. Mum came behind me and tied something around my eyes. Suddenly there was silence. I had no idea what was going on or where she'd gone. Just a deep silence. Then I felt myself floating around the room, with no effort at all and only silence, a breathless silence.

Then the world was still. I realized that I'd stopped flying. I wriggled my hands free and pulled away my blindfold. Mum and Henry were both sitting at the kitchen table. Mum had her face turned away from me.

"Did you see that!" said Henry. "Unbelievable!"

"She really is a witch," Mum said. I could tell she was out of breath. "My own daughter! Imagine!" She burst out laughing.

I untied my feet and lifted Panto up. "You ought to be black," I told her. "I never heard of a witch having a stripy cat before." I still felt strange, very strange. I couldn't quite get the hang of standing up straight. "I think I'll go upstairs and cast a few spells."

I just caught the look in Mum's eyes then, and I knew what it was. She was disappointed. She knew I wanted to e-mail Zed. I'd spoiled everything. I went over to her and said awkwardly, "It's been a lovely evening. Thanks. Thanks for the flying lesson." But it was too late. It was all too late.

· 8 ·

The message said simply: **Maybe it was the ice man.**

Okay, Zed, I typed back. **You've finally flipped.** I looked back to my last message to him. I'd asked him about the man in the battered car days ago. I went and looked out the window. The moon was bright and full. The garden was full of shadows, under the shrubs, on Henry's barbecue patio, by the bird font. But where the clumps of grass had escaped the lawn mower, they seemed to twitch and shiver, to gleam silver like crystal, watchful eyes. The ice man indeed!

It happened the next day. It was Saturday. I had arranged to meet Sandy at the library because we had been paired up to do a history project, and then I was going back to her house for tea. It was to be my treat before the week's work. Mum would be at the studio all week, and I would be looking after the twins. We still hadn't replaced the gormless nanny.

For the first time ever, Sandy was late. It feels strange to look back on all this now and to think that if she'd been on time, none of this might have happened. So, anyway, I picked out the books we needed and one that just caught my fancy: *The Man in the Ice*. I decided to walk on to Sandy's house. I had just left the library when I saw the car again.

I didn't know what to do. I knew, without a doubt, that the driver was looking for me. He had followed me to the library, and he was waiting for me. Now, there were two clear choices. I could have gone back into the library. But the choice I made was to wait at the side of the road, looking up in the direction of Sandy's house. I knew the car had turned around, and when it pulled up just in front of me, I knew the driver had seen me. The passenger door was pushed open.

"Holly? It is Holly, isn't it?"

I nodded, too dumb to speak, too scared, too excited. The driver opened his door and came toward me, half running, half stumbling, lifting his hands and shaking his head and smiling. He stopped and laughed out loud, and his laughter was like a song from ages ago, bringing back all kinds of memories, like when you flick through a photograph album and all your senses come to life: sounds and smells and tastes and touch; voices and music.

"You know who I am, don't you?"

I nodded again, too full of all these other things to trust myself to speak. Anyway, the word was so hard to say, important, huge. I clutched the library books to my chest as if they made a shield.

"I'm your dad."

I nodded again.

"Come and sit in the car. Come and have a coffee somewhere—do you drink coffee? Coke? Want to talk . . . looked everywhere, can't believe . . . little Holly . . . look at you . . . look at you now!"

I don't actually know if he said any of these things. It was just an excited, laughing tumble of words, and I was floating, lighter than last night, when I'd flown in the witch's chair. My throat was so tight that I couldn't manage to say anything, and anyway, I had no idea what to say. I sat in the passenger seat clutching the library books, and he shut the door and ran around to the driver's side. He was still chattering and chuckling, and I still couldn't take in anything.

As soon as he closed the doors, the car smelled familiar. It was a smell of wet dogs and muddy boots, horse feed, leather saddles, hay bales.

"You've changed the car door," I said. We both laughed.

"Like the color?"

The cover of the glove compartment was hanging loose. I did that. I jammed so much inside it one day that it wouldn't close, and I kept pushing till I heard it crack. And he had said—Daddy, as he was then, had said, "Good golly, Miss Holly, you don't know your own strength!"

I tried to put the library books in it. The cover flapped down.

"Good golly, Miss Holly, you broke that years ago!"

I closed my eyes. It was. It really was. It was Daddy.

When I opened my eyes again, I glimpsed Sandy. She

was standing with one hand just raised to wave, a bit unsure of herself, and her other hand was over her mouth as if she was holding fright in. By the time I thought of waving to her, the moment had passed. We were through the traffic lights, and she was left behind: a still, shocked figure in a busy street.

"That was my friend."

"You wanted to talk to her?"

I leaned back. "It doesn't matter. She was late anyway."

It didn't matter. It was true. Nothing mattered now. I was playing a game with new rules. I would have to learn as I went along. There was a language to learn, too. I had no idea what to say. We passed the top of my road, and I blurted out, "I live here."

"Well, we won't go down there then." He laughed, and I laughed, too, and then he pulled up suddenly. The driver behind honked his horn.

"I'm sorry. I mustn't take you for granted. Do you want me to drop you off here?"

I shook my head. My eyes hurt; my throat ached.

"Good." He accelerated. "Very posh, Holly. Your mother's done well."

"She's a television presenter. Well, you've probably seen her."

"Haven't got a telly. A telly star! Imagine that."

"And Henry . . ." I faltered. I had no idea whether my father knew anything about Henry. He glanced at me, raising his eyebrows. "He produces her program," I muttered. I bowed my head. I felt ashamed, deeply ashamed, though I had no idea why. We drove on in a deep, confused silence. Soon we were out of the suburbs and heading toward the motorway.

"Where are we going?"

He laughed again. I think he was nervous, as nervous as I was, but this bubbly laughter kept coming through. I remembered that he always laughed a lot. He was always full of energy and enthusiasm, always wanting to show me things, as if he were another child instead of my father. Funny how I remembered that. I'd never thought about it before.

"I don't suppose it matters. Anywhere. I want to take my girl out for a Coke, and I don't know my way around this place." He jammed his foot on the brake, signaled left, and pulled into the car park of a Happy Eater. "More than a Coke. I think you deserve a hot chocolate. Even a Danish pastry. And I think we should talk. I've got a story to tell you."

· 9 ·

It was hot and steamy in the Happy Eater. Little girls in
long cotton dresses were having a birthday party. They
seemed to be incapable of keeping still. They were hys-
terically jabbering away at one another in what appeared
to be a foreign language. It was impossible to make ourselves heard. I stood next to my father in the queue. He
pointed at a cake that was sticky with glistening raisins
and rolled his eyes as if he was pleading with me to say
yes to it. I grinned and nodded and then found a clean
table for us. I watched him in the queue, raising himself
up onto his toes like a child as he pointed out the cakes
he wanted. I tried to haul together the fragments of
memory that were skittering around my head. I remembered the way he puckered his face as he peered at the
price list. I remembered the way he brought money out
of his pocket and sorted through the coins on the flat of
his hand, how he ducked his head to check where I was,

how he joked with the sleepy lad on the cash till. Full of smiles and excitement, lighting up the room as he wove his way through it, a man who noticed people and made them smile.

"By bon't bike bips," one of the party girls was saying, skipping around my table.

"Bon't boo? By buv bem!" little red pigtail said, bouncing behind her. "By buv bips and beef burgers!"

I cracked the code. I used to play that game with the boy from the farm next door. It used to make me feel as if I had two sets of teeth in my mouth. "By baddy bis buying boo bot bocolates," I said out loud. Red pigtail stopped bouncing and stared at me, twisting her trailing hair ribbon around her wrist. "Band boo bicky bakes!" I added.

She skipped away. "Bicky bakes!" she screamed.

My father sidestepped away from her and swung the tray neatly over her head, like a waiter. He put the tray on the table and beamed at the piled dome of cream on each mug.

"What was the boy next door called?" I asked him. "At the farm?'

"Matthew Tom. Matty. Tall, dark, handsome . . . Wait till you see him."

I bit my lip. Wait till you see him. Mum, I thought, and pushed the thought away.

My father sat down and leaned across to me. He took my hand in both his own. Warm hands, square, working hands. "We've got eight years to make up. I don't know where to start. I've been practicing this meeting for so long that all the words I had in my head have slid down the back of my throat. You start, Holly. Say something, anything, and we'll take it from there. Okay?"

I was silent. I sipped my hot chocolate and licked away my mustache of cream. Words were like flies around a cake; they were like birthday children bouncing and screaming. They made no sense anymore. A long time ago people used to draw pictures on rocks to make sense of their world. It must have been a lot easier.

"I wish you'd written to me," I blurted out. "All that time, and you didn't write. I thought you'd forgotten about me."

My father squeezed my hands. "Good girl. Say it. Say how angry you were."

"Not even at Christmas. Birthdays. Not even a card." I couldn't say any more. Eight years of hurt rolled down my cheeks.

"You're splashing into your hot chocolate," he said gently. "It cost a fortune, too."

I tried to smile. Nothing in my life had ever hurt so much.

He stroked my fingers one by one. I remembered that from long ago, how it used to calm me down when I was upset. His mouth made little, soundless shapes, as if he was trying out things in his head before he said them. I remembered that, too.

"Let me begin at the beginning," he said at last. "I'll tell this story once, and then it's over. It's the past. It's the future I'm interested in, but you deserve to know about the past. And drink your chocolate, it's lovely. I hope you don't mind, but I'm going to dunk my Danish pastry in mine. I love it that way."

I giggled, out of nervousness, out of relief. I was beginning to feel a bit better. He released my hand. The birthday girls were swapping paper hats, shrieking as if it were the funniest thing that had ever happened. A red-faced waitress was trying to clear their plates away. A tired-looking woman shushed them uselessly. I couldn't look at my father while he was talking.

"It was a rainy night, as I'm sure you'll remember. I'd been over to Vincent's about one of the mares I'd sold him. Dixie. D'you remember Dixie? Beautiful, gentle mare. Soft as butter. I used to let you ride her, that's how sweet she was. Well, she was ill, and we were up all night with her, waiting for the vet. I wouldn't leave her. I told your mother I'd be away all night. I wanted to take you. You had a way with horses, an understanding, and Dixie always responded to you. I thought it would calm her to see you, and you could kip down at Vincent's, no problem. Your mother wouldn't let you come. 'You and your horses,' she said. 'You think more of those horses than you do of me.' That's what she said, that day. I'll never forget the way she said that, and how she looked that day, in a loose dress the color of damsons, and that silky hair tumbling down her back like a river. Does she still wear it long?"

I shook my head. I don't think I let my breath go till then.

"Your mother hated the horses. She hated the cottage; she hated the farmyard; she hated the horses. I always knew that. It made no sense to me, but I knew it all the same. I remember how you ran down the lane after me, waving and shouting. We had a chapter of

Tom's Midnight Garden to read. 'Save it till tomorrow!' I shouted. Then we got to the cattle grid, and I couldn't see you anymore, and I started fretting about Dixie. Maybe if I hadn't sold her; maybe if I'd kept her for you . . ."

"But I had Rosa." And I remembered Dixie, though I'd never thought about her till then. She shone like silk, and she was the gentlest and quietest of all the horses. She was the first pony I rode, with Daddy walking along beside us, leading her, coaxing her, coaxing us both.

"Sure, you had Rosa. Anyway, I told your mother I'd be away all night, but it didn't happen that way. Beautiful, brave Dixie died a couple of hours after I arrived. The vet said we'd done everything right, but she just gave up and died on us. So I came home. It was late. I was very tired, very upset. I remember a white car drawing out of the lane as I was driving up to it. Funny, I thought. Have we had visitors, this time of night? The gates had been left open. The cottage was in darkness, door unlocked. I thought you and your mother had gone to bed. I crept upstairs. All the doors were open. Eh, such a silence in the house! I wanted to see you. I always said good night to you. I looked in your room, and I could see your bed in the moonlight, covers thrown back, pillow on the floor. Empty. And the wardrobe door was open, and the drawers underneath, open. I panicked. I ran into the other room. Empty, empty. I went back to your bedroom, and I sat on the bed, and, Holly, I sobbed my heart out. Oh, I knew your mother had stopped loving me. Long, long ago. I knew she hated living there. I half knew, but never wanted to believe, that she had fallen in love with somebody else. But I never dreamed, never, ever, that she would do that to me. That she would just walk out and take you with her. I never thought she'd do that to me."

The birthday girls suddenly erupted past us, dancing in a rippling, boisterous line around the tables. The harassed woman in charge called them to order, flapping her hand like a limp white flag, and they danced out into the car park, taking their chanting with them. They ran past the window, waving to us. Little red pigtail dropped her goody bag.

"She didn't even leave a note. Nothing. Nothing to say why, or who with, or where . . . I remembered the white car. You would have been in it. If only I hadn't been so tired! If only I hadn't been so cut up about Dixie. I should have realized something was wrong when I saw the gates were open, the house in darkness. I should have turned around then and chased that white car. Maybe I could have reasoned with her. I'd have let her go if that was what she really wanted. How could I have stopped her? But I wouldn't have let her take you away."

The chocolate had been served with a plastic spoon. I was letting it float and fall, float and fall, float and fall, into the cream. I balanced it very carefully across the top of the mug. I said, "I didn't want to go. I told him— Henry—I told him I wanted to stay with you." And then I said, "Why didn't you try to find me?"

There was a long silence. "I didn't know where to look. Your grandparents had moved."

I felt I was looking into his hopelessness. "Wasn't

there anything you could do? Couldn't someone have helped?" I was snatching at words. What would Mum have done? "A lawyer? A detective or something?"

He shook his head. It wasn't his way. I knew that.

"Holly, when your mother left, I thought it was my fault. I thought I'd let her down. And I thought I'd let you down, too. I was ashamed. But I knew I'd find you one day."

I looked up quickly. "How did you find me?"

"I had a stroke of luck, Holly. I'll tell you about it one day. Hope I didn't frighten you, following you round like that. Had to make sure."

"We thought you were a prowler. Sandy probably thinks I've been kidnapped."

We both laughed, releasing all that tension. I ate my cake hungrily. My father stole the best bit, the bit I'd been saving. The café was empty suddenly. There was a huge, calm, thinking quiet between us, like a deep ocean, and the memory of our laughter was like the sound of whale songs, far away.

"Actually, that is what I want to do," my father said at last, into that swimming silence. "At first I just thought I wanted to see you. And when I saw you, I thought I just wanted to talk to you. And now I've talked to you, I want you back. It's my turn. Come home with me, Holly."

Home.

I could have asked him to run me back to Whinbush Close so I could explain to Mum. And she would have said no.

The justice of it appealed to me. It was only fair to him.

It was only fair to me. We'd lost eight years of each other. And already we'd stopped being strangers to each other, and I had stopped being a stranger to myself, that other, locked-up self. It was as if I had stepped through a magic mirror, and there I was on the other side, nearly seven years old again, and there was my father with his bright, comical, smiling face and his comfortable well-worn jumper. I knew his hands with their thick, practical fingers. I knew the way he whistled when he was thinking. What else was there to know?

"I've got a pile of letters for you in a shoe box," I told him. "Full of drawings of Rosa."

He stopped whistling suddenly and grabbed my hand. "Come on. Come and see her!"

He ran me out of the Happy Eater so fast that I was shrieking like the birthday girls. He pulled open the car door, the one with the orange paintwork, pushed me inside, and ran around to the driver's side. "There," he said, backing out of his parking spot. "I've done it. I've kidnapped you."

· 10 ·

What we didn't know of course was that my mother was already phoning the police. Sandy had gone back home and fretted and drawn a few pictures and then had told her mother that she'd seen me getting into the battered car that we'd been warned about at school. Her mother, who couldn't stand mine, had got straight into her car and gone around to my house, trembling with horror at the news she was going to have to break.

Dad turned on the car radio. It was playing an Elton John song. He started singing to it, and I knew his lovely, rumbly bass voice. I tried to sing in the same pitch, the way I used to. It tickled my throat to sing so low. It made me cough. But I kept on, coughing and laughing, and he wound down the window so everyone could hear us, singing our heads off, coughing and laughing.

But the music stopped, and the laughing and giddiness. We reached the motorway, and I gazed out the window, gripping my seat till my knuckles hurt. We were going too fast. Everything was too fast, hurtling me into white space. I remember how Julian cried at a party when his balloon burst. That's how I felt then, that the color and the magic and the specialness of the moment had all burst in my face. I asked my father to stop at the next service station. This was wrong. This was all wrong. How could I go away like this, just run away without any clothes or money or anything, just a few library books, no comb or toothbrush or explanation to my mother or anything? He stopped the car, and I looked at him helplessly.

"I'm sorry," I said. "It seemed like a good idea, but can't we—can't we do it some other way?"

"You want me to run you home?"

I nodded. "I think we should talk to Mum."

He drummed his fingers on the driving wheel. He whistled softly between his teeth. "She won't talk to me, Holly. But if you want me to run you home, I'll run you home. I understand. I understand."

I felt like crying. I think I might have been. "It's just that . . . well, I hadn't even thought about it. It's too sudden. I can't just—"

"It's okay."

"I need the ladies' first."

"I'll wait here. It's okay. I understand. Off you go."

I ran across the car park. I couldn't see. My head was hammering; my throat was a tight, fisted ball. I looked back. My father had got out of the car and was walking about on the grass verge of the car park, under the trees.

Inside the washroom a woman was looking at herself in the mirror. She clucked her throat at me and then ducked her head, and as I was going into the cubicle and just looking at her out of the corner of my eye, something very peculiar happened. She took her head off. I shut the door and tried to breathe slowly. I was obviously in a state of distress. The world I knew was dropping into raggedy pieces, and I had no control over anything anymore. Women took off their heads in public places, and fathers kidnapped their own daughters. She was still clucking when I came back out, but this time she was putting her head back on again. I realized that it was a wig. "All right?" she asked, rolling her eyes.

I nodded.

"They get hot and sweaty, these do. Need a bit of air. Bit of hair! Get it? Ooh, I'm a crackpot sometimes!" She chuckled. "Smile, luvvy, you look as if you've got the weight of the world on your shoulders."

I nodded again. I wrung my hands under the dryer.

"Had a row with your boyfriend?"

For some strange reason I remembered Tommy Oliver. Four years ago he had been my boyfriend for a day. It was Rebecca Holloway's birthday party, and we were playing blindman's buff, and it was so daring, so unspeakably exciting, to be kissing a boy. We were all hot with screaming and giggling and running, like the birthday girls in the Happy Eater, but the difference was that there were boys at the party. I was sick with giggling, queuing to be kissed, full of the horror and the mystery of it, and there I was, caught in the arms of Tommy Oliver, smelling his T-shirt and the sardine sandwiches we'd just eaten, and I was as hot as his breath. Every time he was the blindman he lunged at me, tipping his head back to peer up through his blindfold, and his cheeks were red and sticky like toffee apples. "Be my girlfriend," he muttered as we squashed together behind the door and the others screeched around us, and for the rest of the day I was, and the next day he brought me a yo-yo that flashed in the dark but refused to wind itself up. But he was bony and silly and very annoying, and at playtime he asked for his yo-yo back. I don't think I've thought about him since.

"I haven't got a boyfriend yet."

"Lord love you, you're only a child. Make the most of it. When I was your age . . . let's see, was I ever a child? Don't think I ever was. Ma died when I was ten, and I was mother to the six little ones then. No, childhood passed me by. Do I look good? Need a bit of lipstick?"

"You look fine to me."

I washed my face quickly and tried to dry it with the hand dryer. It was like standing in a hot tornado. I fished my Afro comb out of my jeans pocket and tried to get a bit of sense into my hair. The woman looked at me admiringly.

"What I wouldn't give for your head of hair! Ooh, make you seasick, those waves would. Had mine tied up at your age. Goldilocks, imagine! That's what me dad used to call me. 'Tie it up, you're a grown-up woman now,' he told me when Ma died. 'Tie it up out of the way. You've got work to do, Clara Jane.' Not that he wasn't grateful. Little mother, I was. All boys, they was, so I was special. Girls and their dads, that's special, that is.

Don't you think so?" She blew herself a kiss in the mirror and ambled out, patting her wig. Her long velvet coat flowed round her thick ankles like a cloak.

I ran past her into the car park, looking for him, looking for my dad. He was picking up conkers from under the tree, breathing on them, rubbing them on his jumper to make them shine. I touched his elbow.

"I'm coming with you," I said.

And he just nodded, smiled and nodded, stepped away to look at me. "Hey," he said. "Hey. Hey." He put his arms around me and rocked me.

· 11 ·

About an hour later the car broke down. The engine started fizzing and steaming and hissing like an old kettle.

"The gods are against us," Dad said. "But I refuse to break down on the motorway. It costs a fortune to be towed off. Come on, old lady. You can make it." We stayed in the slow lane and juddered on, hemmed between a swaying caravan and a car transporter, our emergency lights flashing, till we got to the next slip road. I had my fingers clenched against the door handle, ready to fling myself out. I thought the car was going to blow up any minute.

We drifted slowly down to a roundabout.

"Left," I suggested. "It's a downhill."

Slowly, agonizingly slowly, we edged our way toward the lights of a village. Yewdale. It was early evening. We had the windows open, and we could hear the cries of owls. Soon it would be completely dark.

"Garage!" Dad shouted suddenly. He swung the car

onto a garage forecourt, and there it died. And he could see, as clearly as I could, that the garage was closed for the weekend.

"Oh, boy." He drummed his fingers on the steering wheel. "Here I am trying to kidnap you and the car breaks down in the middle of nowhere. Is this funny, or is it tragic?"

"It's funny," I told him. "I've got a feeling that this sort of thing is always happening to you."

"Mmm."

"Like the Christmas tree?"

Suddenly I was remembering my last Christmas with Dad. The lights on the tree fizzled out on Christmas morning, and when Dad tried to mend them, all the electricity fused. My mother was angry, flushed, and loud with anger. Dad cooked the meal on the log stove, and it took all day. We ate it by the light of the fire and the oil lamp from the foaling barn.

"It was all right in the end."

"It was lovely," I said. "And the grandparents were there. Nana Zosia." With her deep, strange voice. And the purple hollows like bruises that her eyes sank into. The same color as the lavender that she snips from her garden at the end of the summer. I used to help her push it into muslin bags for the autumn fair, and it smelled sweet and musty on my fingers. And my grandfather—oh, yes, Grandpa Jake I used to call him—Grandpa Jake said, "This lavender stuff is so good I could slip it in my pipe and smoke it!" "Indeed you won't!" Nana Zosia said. "And I'd smell like heaven," he said, and pulled up the side of his face in a big wink at me. When she wasn't looking, he snipped a bunch for himself and slid it inside the brown flakes of tobacco in his pouch. Grunting, bright-haired Grandpa Jake. He used to call me Holly Heartthrob.

"And after the dinner, Nana Zosia sang to us," I said. But it wasn't a song, because there were no words to it, and her poor, bent fingers trembled in the air as if they were plucking notes from nowhere. "So, anyway"—thinking about the Christmas tree lights—"things always turn out well in the end."

"Course they do. Disasters can't be helped, but it's what we make of them that counts. So come on, Holly Starcross. This is our story. Our adventure. Let's find out what happens next." Dad swung down the broken lid of the glove compartment and fished out a torch. Its light wavered feebly. "Oh-oh. Disaster strikes again. Should have bought new batteries!"

I picked up my library books. "I don't want anyone to pinch these. I'd have a massive fine to pay."

He flashed the torch at the titles. "*The Man in the Ice*?"

"Zed told me I should read that."

"Zed? Your boyfriend?"

"Everyone asks me if he's my boyfriend. I don't even know him. We e-mail each other."

"E-mail! Good grief. No, I'm not laughing, I'm full of admiration. I used to have a pen-friend."

"Hmm. The other two are for a history project at school."

"Tell me about school. Come on, we'll walk down to the village and see what we can find. Tell me what subjects you like."

It was nice, walking down that leafy lane with my dad, telling him things about school. He was like a hungry animal, asking me questions, questions all the time, as if everything I told him really mattered. So I told him about the music club at school and how I had joined and started to learn the cello a year ago, at lunchtimes, and soon I would be in the orchestra, and Mum knew nothing about it. I told him how difficult chemistry was, and how I wanted to pack it in when I was old enough. I told him about the new IT block and how we were fund-raising so soon every child in the school would have the use of a computer.

"I've never used one," he said. "I'm not against them. But what does a stable lad need a computer for?"

"Is that what you are?"

"Horse breeder, if you want the posh name. Like your grandpa. And there's nothing like a craft or skill that's lasted, you know, down the centuries. Lived and breathed horses, your grandpa has, like his dad, and his. I never wanted anything else. But you, now, you're in a new world."

Our voices echoed in the dusk. Far away another world roared, cars and lorries on the motorway sighed like a distant sea, but in that lane the only near sound was our voices and the light, brisk clap of our footsteps. I walk like my dad, but I didn't know that till then. I take long, purposeful strides. Last year I used to run, nearly everywhere; walking was just a waste of time. And now I stride. I stride like my father.

"Eh, but fancy you using e-mail." His voice was soft with wonder. "Shooting messages into space. Like putting messages in a bottle. I used to do that on holiday at the seaside. Or tying letters to balloons."

"It's different." I giggled. "With e-mail, you know where they're going."

"Is that right?" I couldn't tell whether he was teasing me or not.

"Well, you don't know where in the *world* they're going, not usually. But you know who they're going to. Except with Zed. I've no idea who Zed is or where. That's the best thing about it."

"So Zed is someone you can say anything to. Like a diary. Or a secret friend."

Yes, I thought. That's exactly what Zed is. And maybe I don't want to know who he really is. Maybe I never will. "And you still haven't got a telly?"

"Nope. Never wanted one."

Little by little I was remembering the silent house, the tick-tocking chiming clock, the crackle of the fire. I remembered hearing the whinnying of horses and the stamping of hooves, the cry of birds, the trilling of the river at night. I had never heard these sounds in my memory before, yet there they were, like a recording of special effects that we used in school plays, just switching themselves on, just like that. Magic. "At home we've all got tellies in our rooms. Well, not Zoe, of course." I felt suddenly shy. I wanted to protect him. "She's the baby."

"Oh yes?" A long silence. "How many more are there?'

Dad, you would love Zoe. "Julian and Lisa. They're twins. They're six."

"I see."

"And a big screen in the living room. I mean really big, like half the wall. It's massive."

"She'll be happy then, your mother."

"Mmm."

"And she can see herself, in her own program. Large as life!"

"She's a good presenter. She talks about things that matter."

"Good." Another long silence. "I think we ought to find somewhere to eat. Looks like a pub coming up." He flicked his nervous torch. "Station Inn. Now that's interesting."

"Trains."

"Trains home," he said. "We'll deal with the car on Monday!"

"There's the platform!" And we ran, laughing mad things, suddenly sure that we could hear a train coming thundering through the dark to whisk us away from this nowhere place. But the platform was deserted, the station was unmanned, and there was no train within sight or sound. The owl hooted again, mocking us. The distant motorway sighed. We peered at a water-stained timetable.

"I can't read a thing," Dad said. "I sat on my reading glasses just before I kidnapped you. Overexcited. You'll have to read me the place-names and see if I recognize anything."

The litany of names sounded like words in a poem. "Brocco Bar, Banner Hill, Silver Cross, Hunters' Edge . . ."

"It's only a local line," Dad said, disappointed. "It doesn't go anywhere useful."

"It must be useful to someone if they live there. They all sound so nice."

"Okay. Pick the nicest, and we'll go there."

"Ringingsands. The end of the line. Ringingsands. Next train comes . . . in fifty minutes."

"We'll have a holiday in Ringingsands. And let's see if the Station Inn can offer us any food. Starving."

"Same here. Could eat a horse."

"I'd rather you didn't say that, Holly."

"Anyway, I'm a veggie."

It was cozy in the pub, with a real fire and chintzy curtains. I had vegetarian bake and chips, and he had a farmer's pie that was swimming in gravy and smelled delicious.

"How come you eat farmers but you don't eat horses?" I asked.

"How come you eat vegetarians?"

The landlady fussed around us, asking questions in a clipped accent that I couldn't understand. The hot food and the fire made me feel sleepy, even though it was only about seven. I would have liked nothing better than to curl up on my own bed for half an hour. In the bar there was a group of people from Liverpool. Their accents were so strong it was almost as if they were speaking a foreign language. A middle-aged man with rusty hair kept leaning forward and relating funny anecdotes. His sweater tightened across his paunch as if he were a pregnant woman. The women with him pealed out their laughter, swaying backward and forward like windblown trees, gale after gusty gale. Their faces were red, and their eyes were watery.

"They're having a good time," Dad said.

I pushed my plate away. "She'll be getting worried, Mum will."

Dad nodded. He forked up the last of his pie.

"I don't suppose you've got a mobile?"

He raised his eyebrows, and we both laughed.

"I think I ought to phone her and tell her I'm okay."

He wiped his mouth and screwed the paper serviette into a little ball. On the table it started to unfold slowly, like a live animal. "She didn't leave me a note. That night she took you away. You could have been dead, both of you. It's taken me *eight* years to find you. One word from you, and she'll be down that motorway to snatch you back. It's up to you."

I turned away from him. Someone at the table next to us lit a cigarette. The smoke hurt my eyes. I knew he was right. Every word was right. But I couldn't bear the thought of Mum frantic with worry. Dad wanted to hurt her. It wasn't fair to use me.

"Just a message to say I'm all right. I don't have to tell her I'm with you."

He spread out his hands, hopelessly. "Do you think for a minute that you'll be able to hear her voice and not tell her?"

He was right. I could imagine Mum demanding, insisting, desperate for reassurance. Then I had a brain wave. When the landlady came fussing and powdery back for her plates I asked her if she had an e-mail address. "I certainly do," she said proudly. "We get most of our hotel customers that way."

"Could I send someone a message? It's really urgent, and I don't have the phone number?"

"Our car's broken down, you see," Dad put in. "We're in a bit of a mess."

"Anything to oblige," the landlady said, fluttery with

interest. "But I can't do it straightaway. This is a busy night. We have the pub quiz at eight."

It would be no use e-mailing home, I knew that. Mum would e-mail straight back and find out where the pub was. I had to be a bit devious. I wrote out a careful message on a scrap of paper. *Dear Zed, I'm on holiday planet with the ice man. Starbeam OK vibes down to murray@aol.com.*

I showed it to Dad. "I don't understand a word of it," he said. "And your mother will think you're on drugs or something."

I shook my head. "She knows me better than that. And Zed will decode it straight. It's just how we talk to each other."

"Fine." Dad handed the message to the landlady, shrugged at her bewildered expression, and then we ran like the wind for the train.

· 12 ·

We were the only people on the platform and the only people in our compartment of the train. When the ticket collector came, Dad bought two to Ringingsands. "Is it nice?" I asked the man.

"Nice?" He rubbed his mustache mournfully. "Depends what you mean by nice." And he wandered away, whistling through his teeth a sharp, sad, tuneless song.

"It's nice," I said.

Dad laughed. "Do you know, for a minute then, the way you looked, you just reminded me of your aunty Margaret when she was your age. Remember her? Must do. My little sister, Maggie."

"Did she have a red dress?"

"Might have done."

"With a swirly skirt. There was a lady with a red dress. She said I could have it when I grew up."

"She was the image of you, with a mop of dark curls, but she wore it shorter than yours, like a cloud of bubbles and always in a tangle. Hopeless tangle. Loads of friends when she was your age. And she got herself a boyfriend when she was about fifteen. Demon Cartwright. His real name was Damian, but he was called Demon by everyone. Suited him. I used to go to school with him. He lived on that farm by the copse, Cartwright's farm. You remember it. The one with all the rusting machinery in the field."

"Dinosaur skeletons."

"Aye, that's what you used to call it."

"I don't remember Demon."

"No. Well, there's a story about Maggie and Demon. There's stories about everyone. You don't know much at all about my side of the family."

He closed his eyes and went so quiet that I thought he'd dropped off to sleep the way Henry does sometimes in front of the television, and then he said, "When they were sixteen, they went joyriding in a stolen car. Had a terrible accident. He was killed. She was unconscious. Took her months to get over it. Just for a bit of fun."

The air in the train was quiet with horror. I thought about the auntie in the red dress who had come to tea one day, and how she had sat quiet and still with her hands folded in her lap like white birds. But when she stood up, her dress had floated around her legs with a *sweesh!* like bright wings unfurling, I put out my hands to touch it, and her face lit up, and she swirled around, just for me, making the skirt billow out. Around she swirled, laughing, with her head back. "Wait till you grow big. I'll save it for you." Then the sun had gone from her face and she was cold again.

"I don't know why I told you all that," Dad said. "It was something else about Maggie that I meant to tell you, seeing you there with your wide-eyed, open face and your eyes full of fun, just like Maggie when she was a kid. But it all came out, all that. Afterward everyone was blaming everyone else for what had happened, but did it help? It didn't. A dead boy and a girl with a broken spirit. People cry when it's too late."

I nodded. I knew why he was telling me this before he said it.

"What I'm trying to say, Holly, is you did right. You did right to send that message to your mother."

· 13 ·

We could taste the salt in the air as soon as we stepped off the train; we could feel the fizz and tang of sand.

"It's the seaside!" I felt like singing, it was such a wonderful surprise. We walked along the windy promenade, gasping as the wind snatched our breath away. Out there beyond the railings the sea was a black and heaving mass, lumbering like a glossy beast along the steel gray sand.

"Closed for the winter," Dad said. "Best time to come to the seaside."

"What if we can't find anywhere to stay?"

"There'll be somewhere. Even if it's a bus shelter."

"I don't think—"

"Joke. I've already seen the twinkling lights of a hotel. But we'll try a B and B first. Fun, eh?"

We came to a house with a B & B sign swinging forlornly over the gate. The Dunes, the house was called. A cat wound itself around my legs as we waited on the doorstep. I picked it up and buried my face in its damp fur. It switched on a luxurious purr.

"Might have fleas."

"Don't care. He reminds me of Panto. Did you know I brought one of the kittens with me when Mum and Henry took me away? She's my favorite thing, next to Zoe."

The Dunes B & B cat jumped out of my arms and shot into the house as soon as the door was opened. An old lady peered out at us. "Closed for the winter," she said.

"Your sign's still up," Dad pointed out.

"Rusted." She was crunching a chocolate digestive biscuit. The crumbs dusted her woolly black chest. Inside the house someone was plonking a piano. A high-pitched, strained voice was having a go at "Ave Maria." There was a gust of warm radiator air.

"I'm really sorry. It's just for one night. A couple of rooms for me and my daughter. It would be lovely here." Dad's voice was wistful and persuasive. I don't think even Mum could have turned him down.

I put in my bit. "It's perfect, looking over the sea."

She took another bite of biscuit. Another drift of crumbs floated down. "Can't be bothered with one-nighters."

"We'll stay for two nights and pay you for three, in advance." Dad spoke it like a conjuring trick. "And this girl doesn't even eat bacon."

The woman chuckled in spite of herself, puffing up a cloud of crumb dust. "Come on then. Where's your luggage?"

Dad explained that we were on our way home and that our car had broken down. "We can't pick it up till Monday, so we decided to have a holiday at the seaside."

"So you've no nightclothes and no toothbrushes and no nothing," she said.

"We'll manage."

She grunted and clumped up the stairs in front of us. She was wearing ankle socks that were disappearing inside the heels of her slippers. She pointed out two rooms that had flowers capering over the walls, the bedspreads, the lampshades, and the curtains. "You can sit downstairs and watch telly while I make up the beds. I see you're a bookie type, though." She cocked her head sideways to read the spines of my library books. "Can't get going on books myself. Too many words. And I'll get her to give you a cup of tea. She's been thumping that piano for hours, and she hasn't got a decent tune out of it yet. Years actually, if the truth be told." She chuckled again in a knowing, conspiratorial way and ushered us back downstairs.

The television lounge had an electric fire with a flickering flame effect and a huge, smothering pink settee. We collapsed into it, giggling, as she went into another room to halt the pianist. There was a flurry of animated conversation and then silence. We wondered if they'd both gone out.

"Tell me another story," I said.

"Who would you like to know about?"

"Grandpa Jake," I said firmly. "I can't remember him properly, except how nice he was. I know lots about Mum's dad, Granddad Douglas. He made me laugh a lot. And he was always telling me stories about when he was a soldier in the war and showing me his medals."

"I liked your Granddad Douglas. He never had much time for me, though. Country boy. Not good enough. I didn't know him very well. But your grand-dad Bill Douglas and your grandpa Jake Starcross couldn't have been more different if they'd come from different planets. Banker and horseman. Southerner and northerner. Public school boy and country lad. They never met. I don't think they'd have understood a word if they'd tried to have a conversation. And you're the flower that comes from both those trees, Holly. Don't forget that. There's a bit of both sides in you."

I thought about this. Where did the *real me* start? I knew I had lots of Grandma Douglas in me. "Grandma reads all the time, and if anyone's around, she'll read out loud to them. I'm like that. I love stories. Always, always. Mum doesn't. So maybe I caught reading off her. And Granddad Douglas—well, he hated sprouts, and so do I."

Dad laughed. "Holly Starcross, you're a wonderful girl, d'you know that? No wonder I've missed you so much! Well, all right, I'll tell you a story about Grandpa Jake, seeing as you're going to meet him again soon and stare into his whiskery old face and his misty eyes. I'll tell you something about the kind of boy he was. Let's see . . . he'd be about fifteen. Can you see him? Same curly hair as you and me. Brown eyes. Skinny lad—he was never big. And he was the only son, so he had to help his mother on the farm. You won't remember your great-grandmother Matilda Starcross, widowed at twenty, strongest woman in the valley, prided herself on being as good as any man. Better, sorry. Better. Was, by all accounts. Rode everywhere on a great black mare called Martha. And I remember her in stout boots and a long, thick sort of army greatcoat that must have belonged to her husband, nearly threadbare with wear, and a red head scarf. Tough as a workhorse, and a big, loud voice that carried over any wind when she was rounding up the sheep or the horses—aye, we had sheep on the farm in her day. Leathery brown cheeks—I can see her now. So, her husband, your great-grandfather, was long dead, and she and young, skinny Jake ran the farm together."

At that point the door was pushed open, and a red-headed, spindly version of the landlady came in with a tray of tea and digestive biscuits—plain ones, I was disappointed to see. She peered at me full in the face as if she were trying to see how many blackheads I had, then dumped the tray on the nasty little glass table and backed out.

"Thanks," Dad called after her. "Very kind."

" 'Snothing, love," came the landlady's voice. We heard the two of them whispering fiercely on the other side of the door.

"Go on," I said. I dunked a biscuit into my cup of tea and sucked it. Delicious, to be able to do that and to know that I wasn't going to be told off for it. In fact, Dad did exactly the same thing.

"Well, fifteen-year-old Jake had a fond heart for a farm lass that he met at a country fair, over Glossop. Good fifteen miles away, over the top. Just before Christmas one year he wanted to step over and give her a poppy red scarf. He set off in bad weather, and a snow-storm blew up. He didn't turn up, and she looked at the weather and thought, No wonder. And he didn't turn up home for bed, and my grandmother thought he must be stowed away for the night under the kitchen table at the big farm. He didn't come home the next day, and she thought of striding over to the farm and fetching him home, love or no love, because there was work to do. But evening drew on, and she began to worry for him. So what did she do but set off up that steep track behind the house, calling for her lost lad. She found his footsteps in the snow, deep, weary trudges of them, and she fol-lowed them till she knew the story they told. He'd got himself lost and had wandered around and around like a ship in a gale, and all the stars put out with the snow. She found the red scarf, and there he was, tucked into some stones. There was no leaving him there, was there, alive or dead? So she hoisted him onto her back and plowed her way across those snowy moors with him. I'm talking about miles, on a hard winter's night. That's a mother's love for you."

How quiet we both felt when Dad said that.

He dunked the last digestive biscuit. His tea must have been cold by then, but he drank it down as if he had a great thirst.

"Did he ever see the girl again?"

"What?" He put his cup down and laughed. "I call that a happy ending, don't you? No, I don't know any more about the lass from Glossop. His next love affair wasn't for ten whole years, when Zosia Kobel came to ride one of the horses. But I'll tell you about her another day. Your eyes are about disappearing in the back of your head. Off you go, Holly. Off to bed." He held my hand and kissed it, the way he used to do a long time ago when I was Sleeping Beauty and he was the handsome prince waking me up for my breakfast. "Sweet dreams, princess."

I did have dreams. They were about the ice man again. This time he was covered with snow, and I wiped him with a poppy red scarf and then just lifted away his face. It was a perfect mask of ice, and when I put it over my face, it fitted.

· 14 ·

The next day, Sunday, was my best day ever. There it was, the sea. Far away a tiny white boat, coming from a magic place. We walked along the marine wall to the next village, and we never stopped talking. Dad gave me one of his gloves, and he wore the other one, and we walked really fast, swinging our arms to keep warm. The sky was the sort of brilliant blue that you see only on picture postcards, and the sea sparkled right to the horizon, and over it, I suppose, sparkling like tinsel for hundreds of miles. Seagulls cruised over it as if they had no weight at all, bits of white paper cut-out birds, except every now and again they opened their throats and sobbed for sheer joy.

"They love being seagulls, don't they?" I said. "You can tell."

"Awful singers, though. Do you remember the skylark's song? Over the moors at home, just about filling the sky with music?"

"No. I don't think so."

"Wait till you hear that song, Holly Starcross. They must be happy, to sing like that. If you were a bird, that's what you'd be, I reckon."

"Would you be a skylark, too?"

"Me? A heron. A great clumsy, ancient, mysterious heron, standing about all day looking into the water. And taking off—wow, when it takes off, you should see it! Great gray-blue wings, like a ghost rising out of the reed banks, like an angel. I think it's some kind of dinosaur bird. Has to be.'

"Does it sing?'

"Nope. *Kaaark,* it goes. *Kaaark.* No song. Not what you'd call a song anyway. I like that. If I were a musical instrument, I'd make that sort of sound, whatever I was. Perhaps I'd be a trumpet and not very well played. What about you?"

"Cello." No doubt about that. Beautiful, deep-voiced, singing cello. I thought of my school cello, snug in its brown leather coat in the instrument room. It almost *is* human to look at.

"Ah-ah," Dad said. "Cello. That reminds me of a story. Fancy some chips?"

We ran to the fish-and-chips shop. Nothing in the world smells as good as fish-and-chips eaten outside. We each kept a glove on and ate the chips with the free hand. We sat on the seawall, with our legs dangling over the creamy waves, and threw batter bits to the screaming gulls. We could see a few windsurfers in wet suits skimming like bright balloons across the water. I liked it best when they fell in. And while we were eating and watching, Dad told me the story of Zosia and Jake.

"As I said before, my dad, Jake, was a country boy brought up to country ways. Never traveled further than he could walk or ride. Loved horses to a passion, and that's something I caught off him.

"Well, one day, four young men and women came in from town for a ride. They were foreigners. Two men, two women. Only one of them spoke English, and her name was Zosia. Jake had never met anyone like her before. She told Jake that they were a group of musicians touring Europe. After touring England, they were traveling to France and Italy, then back home to Austria. You know what I'm going to say."

"They fell in love."

"They did. Zosia came every day with her friends, and one day she came on her own. She and Jake rode right up to the moors together, and he felt he had never been happier. He thought his happiness was going to last forever. That's what it's like when you're in love. And suddenly it all powdered into tiny flecks of ash, floating away. One minute he had everything he wanted in the world, and the next it was being snatched away from him. Her tour in England had finished. But Jake found he couldn't live without her. He wasn't eating; he wasn't sleeping; he walked the moors by moonlight, and at dawn he lay staring at the cobwebs fluttering from the beams on his bedroom ceiling. His mother didn't know what to do with him. Having saved his life once, she realized she was going to have to do it again. She gave him her savings and told him to stay away till he'd found his girl again."

I must have stopped eating, I was so wrapped up in the story. Next thing I knew, a great herring gull as big as a dog flew down and pinched a chip out of my hand. I nearly toppled off the seawall with shock. Dad swung his arm across me and pulled me back into place. He gave me one of his chips.

"So Jake set off with both his pockets jingling. He'd never been further than Bakewell until then. To Paris! Not a word of *parlez-vous* in his head. You have to be proud of the old lad.

"When he was there, he looked at all the billboards and found the name of Zosia's orchestra. But they'd already moved on! They'd moved on, and moved on, and wherever he went he was too late, and he'd always just missed them. In the end he reached Vienna. He heard a band playing and saw someone in it who looked just like Zosia! He called out to her, and she ignored him. Imagine! He walked away, but she sent someone after him who could speak English.

" 'I have a cousin called Zosia,' she told him. 'Is this the Zosia you look for? Zosia is sad because she loves an Englishman. Are you that man? Are you the man with the horses?' "

"Oh, Dad!" My chip paper was a greasy, cold ball in my hand, completely forgotten about. "So he found his Zosia?"

"They took him over the mountains to where she lived. As they came to the house, they could hear her playing, such sweet, sad music that it would fill your heart to hear it. There they left him. And I leave it to your imagination to picture the scene as Jake knocked on the door and Zosia put down her music and came to answer him."

"Oh, wow! And she married him."

"Of course."

"And she's my nana Zosia!" I could picture her, dark eyes ringed with purple, and the strange way she spoke her words, and her fluttering hands. Little Nana. "Little Nana, I used to call her!"

Dad nodded.

"But what about her music?"

"Jake worked for local farmers. But he was never happy away from England. Zosia's orchestra was very good, but they were amateurs, traveling around Europe after the war on a cultural exchange. She was really a teacher. She loved teaching more than performing."

"So he brought her home."

"Exactly. She took up teaching locally, and he was back with his beloved horses. Bit like a fairy story, eh? But something even stranger than magic can make things like that happen sometimes. Maybe fairy stories are about real wishes that came true." Dad jumped down from the wall. "Let's walk on. I've got a numb bum."

I jumped down, too, and jogged about on the spot to bring my circulation back. I kept thinking about dark-eyed little Nana, sitting quietly in a corner, her fingers fidgeting in empty air.

"To think it was my own grandparents! Fancy them having a romantic story like that!"

"People are never quite what you think they are," said Dad. "And everyone's got a story to tell. I'm getting cold. Shall we start back?"

I had to lengthen my stride almost to a run to keep up with him. He had his head down, and he was striding quickly, flapping his arms against his sides to try to keep warm. He was beginning to look like his heron, in his long gray coat and his pale scarf.

I was still lost in the story. It was magic. It was as magic as my dad turning up at my school just like that and finding me.

· 15 ·

Before we went back to the B & B that night, we stopped at a seedy-looking Indian restaurant for a curry. A yawning waiter who looked as if he'd just woken up brought us the menu. Dad peered at it.

"You'll have to help me with this, I can't read it. Does that say madras?"

"Madras is very hot," I told him. "You don't want madras."

"Don't I?"

"You'll have steam coming out of your ears. I don't want the responsibility. That waiter might throw water over you."

"You choose for me then." He pushed the menu over toward me. The yawning waiter came back with some pappadams.

"And don't crunch these so loudly," I told Dad. "We don't want to attract too much attention."

He flipped the menu card as if he were slapping my cheeks with it. "Have you enjoyed today?"

"Fantastic. Best yet!"

When we got back to the B & B, we let ourselves in and went up to our rooms. I had a shower, though I had no clean clothes to change into. Perhaps we'd be able to buy some tomorrow. Then I realized that we'd never actually talked about where we would be tomorrow or when I might be going home. My real home. I pushed that thought into a little drawer in my head and shut it fast.

Dad followed me downstairs to the lounge and switched on the electric fire, and immediately the landlady came into the room. I was disappointed to see that she wasn't carrying a tray of hot drinks. She tugged the curtain across, and now there was a husband, whom we'd never seen before. He hovered in the doorway, whistling softly under his breath. The spindle piano player propped herself against the wall behind him.

"What did you say your name was?" the landlady asked suddenly, thrusting her face so close to mine that I could smell the biscuits and tea on her breath.

Before I had time to answer, Dad said, "I don't think we did. Elliott. I'm Peter, and my daughter is Alice."

I shut my mouth quickly.

"Alice," repeated the landlady softly. "I thought I heard you call her Holly, or something like that."

Dad laughed his easy, friendly laugh. "Lally," he said. "It's a pet name. She could never manage Alice when she was little."

I braved a smile, and so did the landlady. In the doorway, the husband sighed and jingled the coins in his pockets. The spindle folded herself up and crept into their private room.

"We've had a long day," I said, yawning to prove it. "We've walked miles. Gosh, I'm thirsty!"

The landlady kept on staring at me, as if there was something really interesting about my face. I smiled at her.

"No chance of a cup of tea, I suppose?" said Dad. "Early night for us?"

"I'll see what I can do." She switched her gaze to him, then back to me. "You're very alike," she said at last, and went out. From behind the closed private door we heard the husband giving a brief, pleased laugh.

"What was all that about?" I whispered. "*Lally?* For goodness' sake!"

"I'm not sure. I didn't know I was such a good liar, but I just said the first thing that came into my head. If she asks you anything else, try to tone down your posh accent. You're a Derbyshire lass, remember."

"Got you," I said. I tried it again, in Derbyshire. It was too hard. When the landlady came in again, I just sat with my head buried in a sailing magazine.

Dad chatted about seals, of all things. "Do you ever get them round here? We live in the middle of the countryside. Lally's never seen a seal. Badgers and weasels, yes, foxes, but never seals."

The husband was hovering again. I knew he was watching me. I pretended to flick through the pages casually, but my hands were shaking. And I suddenly thought about my books upstairs, with the name of the library stamped across the borrowers' pages. Dead give-away. I ran upstairs to hide them. I was sure they'd been moved. I hid them under my jacket, but it looked suspicious, so I tucked them under my arm and strolled down the stairs casually. Mr. and Mrs. Doubtful and their skinny daughter, Spindle Spy, were huddled in the kitchen, bobbly-colored blurs behind the glass, whispering furiously. In the lounge Dad had switched on the television.

"I think I'll go to bed," I told him. "I don't know why, but I feel really nervous."

"I think we ought to watch the news."

It was the fifth item. My mother's photograph was flashed on the screen. I nearly passed out with surprise. Then a shivering woman reporter was on, standing outside our school gates. "The search continues for television celebrity Diane Murray's missing fourteen-year-old daughter, Holly. She was last seen getting inside an old saloon car, and the driver is wanted for questioning. As yet no ransom has been sought." And then came my school photograph, unmistakably me: dark, curly hair, brown eyes, halfway into a shy, lopsided smile. You could just see a bit of Sandy next to me, broad, cheeky grin on her face. My heart turned over and over in slow revolutions. How many times had I seen photographs like this on the television screen, and terrible lines of policemen searching fields in the dark, and mothers breaking down in front of the camera. Dad switched off the television quickly. He sank down onto the settee. I sat next to him, and we both stared at the blank screen in complete silence.

94 •

We could hear the television now in the opposite room. We could hear the raised voices of the landlady and her husband, his reasoning and joking, hers tight, with a slight sharp edge of fear in it. Dad put his head in his hands. "You'd better go upstairs," he said, "before she comes in to have another look at you. We'll leave before breakfast tomorrow."

I ran upstairs, my heart thudding, clutching my library books against my chest. The private door opened. "Holly?" the landlady called. I ignored her. I ran straight into my room and closed the door. I stood in the dark with my back against it. I didn't know what to do. When at last I put the light on, I could see myself in the dressing table mirror, a frightened child, my face white, my eyes huge with fright, my mass of curly hair like a wild dark cloud around my head. It was unmistakably the face that had just stared at me from the television screen.

"Alice has gone to bed," I heard Dad say. "I've walked her off her feet today. Don't bother cooking for us tomorrow. We need an early start."

"I'll leave the cereals out." Her voice was quiet with doubt. "And some fruit. You can help yourselves. Where was it you said you're going?"

"Not quite decided," Dad said. He started to climb the stairs. "Thank you for putting us up at such short notice. I'll bring all the family next time. Good night now."

He ran lightly up the stairs, whistling, as if he hadn't a care in the world. There wasn't a sound from downstairs now. I imagined them grouped in the hall, their ears strained, their thoughts wide open, the landlady standing with her hand on her biscuity chest, biting her lip. I heard Dad go into his room. I didn't move. I was still stunned at the sight of my own face staring out at me from the television screen.

A couple of moments later Dad tapped on my door. "Alice? Can I come in?" He took one look at me and put his arms around me. I struggled free.

"I need to phone Mum," I mumbled. "She'll be out of her mind."

He didn't say anything.

"You're just playing a game with me," I said. I couldn't help saying it. I wanted to hurt him. "You're just wanting to get your own back on Mum. You're using me."

Dad crossed over to the window. He pulled back the curtain and opened the window, wide. The sound of the sea came surging in, deep, calm, long, slow, steady breaths. "As soon as she knows where you are, she'll want you back." I could hardly hear his voice. "I know your mother. She won't negotiate. I'll lose you." He turned around, and I could see that his face was white, too, and his eyes were deep in their sockets. "I just want you for a bit longer. That's all I'm asking."

"I know." I could hardly swallow.

"We had a lovely time today. Eh? Just a few more days like today. That's all."

I put on my jacket. My hands were shaking; I couldn't do it up. I picked up the library books, hugging them to me.

"When she took you away from me like that, she did the wickedest thing a wife could do. If you'd been killed in a car accident, it couldn't have been worse. I've searched and searched for you. I've never given up. You're my daughter. *I* want you, too."

I was frightened. I'd never heard anyone so full of emotion before.

"I did want to punish your mother, yes. Not now. I just want more time with you."

"I want to ring Mum," I said quietly.

"Okay."

"I haven't any money."

"Okay."

Dad went into his room and came back with his coat on. "It suits you," I wanted to say. "You look like a heron." It was a real Dad coat. It was the nicest coat I'd ever seen. Instead I said, "I must be the only child in England who doesn't have a mobile."

He followed me out of the room and dropped the key on the glass hall table. It had a white painted rose cut into it, and twisted gold legs. He followed me down the road, whistling softly, and I knew he was there to protect me and support me, not to make me say anything I didn't want to say. When I went into the telephone box, he stood out of earshot, hands in his pockets, looking out at the heaving, invisible sea.

It was Henry who answered the phone. My heart stopped beating when I heard his voice. I looked out at Dad, just a dim shape at the end of the street.

"It's Holly," I said. I wanted to cry.

I could hear the relief flooding his voice. "Holly? Where are you? Are you all right? Diane, Diane, it's Holly! Are you all right?"

I could hear him walking up the stairs with the

phone. We have bare wood, and the boards echo. I could picture the house with all its clean, shining wood and soft lights. I could picture Mum coming running to take the phone from him. "Holly! Are you all right?"

"I'm fine. I'm really fine." I had to keep swallowing. "I'm sorry you were worried."

"Where on earth . . . ?"

"You don't have to worry about me." I took a deep breath. "I'll be home in a few days."

I tried to talk steadily over my mother's voice. I could hear her moving from anxiety to relief to anger. "Where are you? What on earth is going on, Holly? That silly e-mail came— Who *is* this Zed? Are you with him?"

I looked at Dad again. He was blowing into his hands. I had both his gloves in my pocket now. "Bye, Mum. I'll see you in a couple of days."

I put the phone down. I could still hear Mum's voice in my head, broken off, a cry of anger or grief silenced just like that and still going on all those miles away in our house. A butterfly moves its wings, and thousands of miles away a hurricane starts, they say. I wanted to sob my heart out. Dad turned as soon as I came out of the telephone box. He put his arm around me and I put my head on his shoulder. "I didn't tell her."

· 16 ·

We started to walk, his arm still around me. I felt warm and wanted. I felt better.

"I just said I'd be home in a couple of days. I don't want to go home yet."

"Holly, you're a star. You're a real star." He took both my hands in his and swirled me around, laughing. "Now, think quick. What next?"

"I suppose Mum might phone the police."

"Bound to. They'll trace the call."

"The landlady's probably phoned them already."

"Out of here."

"Station!"

He started to run, pulling me with him. We were both laughing.

"Don't attract attention!" I tried to pull him back.

"Okay. I was out of breath anyway. But walk fast."

The station was deserted. "You'll have to read the timetable," Dad said. "I—"

"Sat on your glasses. I know. You're a disaster." I peered at the tiny writing. "Sunday service. There's none going back to Yewdale."

"We don't want to go there. Your friend spotted the car, remember. The police are looking for it. Anyway, it . . ."

"Doesn't work," we said at the same time. It was very funny. We both felt hysterical with laughing.

"So somewhere else . . . There's one in fifteen minutes! The last train! And it only stops at a place called Newton."

"Could be anywhere."

"Probably is. Okay. So we go to Newton and arrive in the middle of the night. That's fine."

Dad tutted. "Or we go back to our nice, comfy beds at Mrs. Inquisitor's, have a lovely breakfast tomorrow without bacon or sprouts, stroll down to the station, get the car fixed, and drive home. That's the most sensible thing."

"Of course it is. There's no competition, is there?" I sat down on a freezing cold bench and Dad sat next to me.

"Cold?"

"I'm okay. You could tell me a story. While we're waiting."

"Okay. Real or pretend?"

"Real. I like them best. Tell me one about you."

"Age?"

"Sixteen."

"Aha!" He laughed. "You wouldn't have thought much of me at sixteen. Neither did my mum! There were only two things I was interested in, horses and my guitar."

"Guitar! I didn't know you played guitar."

"I thought I was pretty good. I don't think my mum did, though! I had a band—me and Vincent—he was drums, Jody Tom on bass, and a lad called Hairy Michael on vocals. Hairy Michael thought we were going places. I suppose we all did."

"Did you do gigs?"

"Only to the cows on Jody's farm. We used to practice in a barn, where no one else could hear us. But Hairy Michael wanted to get us on big time. He put us in for a talent competition."

"Did you win?"

"Well, we had to go through a couple of rounds, and to our amazement it was a walkover. Actually Hairy Michael was pretty good, he wrote the vocals, too, and they were all pretty snappy. So we got to the finals. They were held in town at the city hall. Two thousand people there! I just wanted to lock myself in the toilets and hope they'd go on without me. Hairy Michael was striding up and down in the greenroom, as they call it, giving us a pep talk. We were going to be stars; we were going to take the world by storm; we were on the first rung to the big time."

Dad stood up. There was a distant humming sound. "Train's coming. Are you sure about this? You can change your mind yet."

"If we go back, we might be captured." We both laughed at the word.

There weren't many people in the compartment. A woman sitting opposite us slept with her mouth wide open. She was surrounded by bulging carrier bags.

"Go on," I said. "*Did* you win?"

The conductor came for the tickets, and Dad bought two singles to Newton. "Is there a hotel there, d'you know?" The sleeping woman snapped her eyes open and stared at us. The conductor shook his head.

"Nothing there. Search me why anybody goes there. Go somewhere else. Nobody goes to Newton except commuters and truckers." The woman switched her gaze to him, then yawned stickily and closed her eyes again.

"Okay. That's fine," said Dad. "Fine." He folded his hand over mine.

"It doesn't matter," I whispered. "Something will turn up. Go on with the story."

He whistled for a bit as if he was deep in thought about something. I squeezed his hand.

"Mmm? Right-o. When we walked onto that stage, my legs were shaking and my fingers were sticking to the guitar as if they were lumps of chewing gum. Half our school was there, cheering us. They'd hired a coach to come. As soon as we started playing, Vincent's drumsticks flew out of his hands! Jody started off in the wrong key and just stood there with his mouth hanging open, watching my fingers to try and sort out what chords I was playing, which wasn't much use because I was all over the place. And Hairy Michael—he saved the day. He just carried on singing as if all our messing about were part of the act. He was brilliant. The crowd loved him."

"And did you *win*?"

"We came second to a ten-year-old tap dancer in a sailor suit."

The woman with the bags burst out laughing. Her eyes were still closed.

"But I loved it, Holly, once I'd got my courage back. Hearing the crowd enjoying themselves and cheering us when we'd finished. Wasn't about winning in the end. Just knowing we could make people enjoy themselves. Bit special that. No, I can't call myself a musician, not me. Not like your nana Zosia. But it was all fun, those days with the band. Brilliant."

I could feel my head nodding against Dad's shoulder. He put his arm around me to make me comfortable, and the next thing I knew, the train was pulling to a halt.

"Wake up, love. We're here."

I rubbed my eyes. Yes, I was awake, but I had been somewhere else, in a crowded hall of cheering people. It appeared I had just done something wonderful, but I didn't know what it was. I followed Dad and the other passengers off the train. The woman with the carrier bags suddenly came back to life and scrambled out, dropping her scarf, her bag, some apples, and a bag of bread cakes onto the platform. Dad helped her pick them up. I gazed around me, shivering, as the people of my dreams slipped into the shadows and disappeared forever. Dad put his arms around me and rubbed my shoulders to warm me up.

"It's been a long day, and I don't know when it's going to end. Trust me still?"

I nodded, yawning hugely again and again.

The woman with the carrier bags scampered past us down the ramp and leaped into the only taxi. Dad ran after her and tapped on the glass just as the driver was beginning to reverse. He shook his head, but Dad opened the door anyway.

"I just want to make sure you're coming back. My daughter's too tired to walk anywhere."

"Maybe we could drop you somewhere," the woman said. She had a husky, warm Scottish accent. "I'm going quite a long way."

"You're very kind." Dad was already pushing me in. The driver tutted.

"We're looking for the truckers' cafe," Dad said. "Does it have rooms?"

"Egg and chips!" I mumbled. Then I felt my head nodding against the delicious padding of the Scottish woman's shoulder, and I slid down into the rocking sea of sleep. When I woke up again, Dad was paying the taxi driver and the woman was hoisting her bags of shopping from under my legs.

"Come on, pet," she said. "You're getting out here."

I was very confused. "Are you Zosia?" I asked, realizing my mistake as soon as I'd said it.

"Zosia?" The woman laughed. "I'm Andrea McPherson."

The taxi drew away like a ship in the night. The dark shapes of conifer trees bowed their heads above us.

"She's our fairy godmother," Dad said. "Mrs. McPherson has kindly offered us beds for the night." He picked up some of her carrier bags and followed her up the drive. I scrunched after them.

"We could be murderers."

"You don't look like murderers. You look like a very tired child in need of a good night's sleep. Zosia,

though"—she chuckled—"I rather fancy that name."
She let us into the bright, flower-filled house and led us
through to a huge kitchen. The fridge was muttering
away to itself. She let her carrier bags sink onto the
floor, where they settled into sleeping shapes like little
plastic animals. "There's plenty of spare beds here," she
said. "It's a home for the elderly, but we're a bit quiet at
the moment."

She guided me down a carpeted corridor that had
soft night-lights glowing, and into a pink room with a
tidy bed and the quilt folded back for me to climb
straight in. There was even a worn teddy bear on the pillow, and as I cuddled him up to me, I wondered if he had
been brought in by a resident who hadn't been able to
part with him for ninety years.

· 17 ·

Next morning we helped ourselves to breakfast in the kitchen, as Mrs. McPherson was busy with the residents. We could hear the clatter of cutlery in the next room and the high hum of voices. Someone started to play the piano. I was finishing my fourth round of toast and marmalade when Mrs. McPherson came in with a trolley loaded with used crockery. The piano started again, deep, full chords. It sounded ever so sad. Mrs. McPherson sighed. "There goes Chopin again. It's all he wants to do all day, and he knows he's not allowed before ten. He's very naughty."

"It sounds lovely," I said.

"Alice plays the cello," Dad said, proud. "Like her grandmother."

"I wish I did play like her. I only just started a year ago." I stood up quickly and scooped toast crumbs into my hand. My cheeks were flaming. I hate this, I thought. I hate hiding. I hate calling myself Alice.

Dad came over and just squeezed my shoulder, and I knew he'd heard my thoughts as if I'd shouted them out at the top of my voice. "We'd better go. We'll make our way to the transport caff and see if we can pick up a lift. This girl's got to get to school." He ruffled my hair, and I dodged away from him.

"She's a lovely girl," Mrs. McPherson said. "We had a girl like Alice, and we lost her."

Her voice was suddenly soft and full. Her eyes brimmed. I looked at Dad quickly.

"But golden. Golden as the sun. We lost her. Went on a school trip and never came home. Coach crash. Wet road. Died instantly. We gave up. Left. Came here. Takes our minds off it, busy. Long time ago now. There. All got stories, haven't we? All had lives."

She smiled. Her eyes were still full. "It's been lovely having you here, father and daughter, so close. Lovely to see that. Good luck to you both."

We walked away from the house with Mrs. McPherson's story singing like sad music inside us. She is one of my special people, though I'll probably never see her again in my life.

"Wasn't she kind?" I said to Dad.

And he said, "Some people are like that. They've so much to give, even though they've lost so much themselves. You meet them and they go away, but they touch your life somehow. I met someone else a bit like that when you were born. Do you know that story?"

"I know I was nearly born in the car!" I giggled. "Mum's often told me that."

"Aye, and she probably blames me for it."

"She does."

"Well, it's a good story, and I'll tell it to you some-time." He stopped, staring into a photographer's win-dow. It was full of wedding photographs. "We throw things away so easily these days. We throw people away as if they were empty Coke cans. The world is littered with the garbage of broken marriages."

"Dad—" Please stop, I wanted to say. It's my hurt, too. Instead I said, "Do you need a shave, Dad?"

He rubbed his chin ruefully. "I do."

"You look like a ruffian."

"Do I? I thought I looked rather handsome. Like a pirate."

"We'll have to do something about it."

He pointed to a store that had a SALE sign in the win-dow. "Fancy some new clothes?"

"You mean a disguise?"

"I do. I give you fifteen minutes to change your identity. Anything you like. But, Holly—no haircut! You've got beautiful hair."

First time anyone had ever said *that*! Now this was a challenge. Anyone who sees me once knows me a sec-ond time because of my hair. It's wild, I mean wild. It's so thick and long and curly. Mum would love me to have it cut, but I've resisted her every time she mentions it, and Henry has always backed me up. At school I have to wear it in tight, tight braids.

It wasn't a department store, after all. Newton was too small for that. It was a household and gardening shop, but it did have an outdoor clothes section. It took me two minutes to make my choice because there was no choice. I was wearing a pair of blue jeans, a black roll-neck jersey sweater, and a black corduroy jacket with a mock fur collar that Grandma Murray had bought me. Very smart. And black buttoned boots. I bought a pair of dark green fleecy tracksuit trousers, a navy blue sweatshirt with a row of sheep ambling across the chest, a green fleece top with a zip and a hood, and a fleecy hiking hat—it was royal blue and dark purple, and it was much nicer than it sounds, with plenty of room to pile my hair in—a pair of lightweight walking shoes in green with a purple strip along the side, and some blue gloves. Then I picked up a small green-and-black rucksack to put my old clothes in. I went to the pay desk and couldn't see Dad. A man in a thick, navy blue fisherman's knit sweater and olive combat trousers turned around. We stared at each other and laughed. I picked up an olive green hat with earflaps and handed it to him.

"I needed some new clothes," he said, "but I couldn't have gone for a complete identity change. I haven't worn a suit since my wedding day, and look what a disaster that was." He stuffed his wonderful, comfortable multicolored jumper, his flappy worn cords, and his old heron coat into a carrier bag and paid for the lot with a credit card. "Are you happy in that person?"

"Really comfy," I said. "And warm. And Mum would disown me!"

"That's the main thing."

I felt wonderfully happy. I can't tell you how good it felt to have my city gear stuffed in a bag on my back and to be wearing these bright, cheerful country clothes. Of course I found out later that country people don't really wear those kinds of clothes. It's only city people who are going out to the country for the day who dress up like that. But anyway, no one I knew had ever appeared in public in such a getup. I felt as if I were dressed for a part in a play, ready to learn the lines and the plot. I didn't know how the play was going to end. *Ghostly!* One day I would know where home was. But for today, and tomorrow, and even, wish against wish, the next day, I was Dad's. Dad's girl.

· 18 ·

"Now I'm going to ring that garage," Dad said. "If they think they've got an abandoned car there, they'll be notifying the police in no time."

While Dad was making the phone call, I browsed through some magazines in a newspaper shop. I nearly bought one that had a free body glow stick offer. For a moment I saw myself and Sandy painting ourselves with it, laughing in front of her bedroom mirror, turning off the light to see ourselves glowing in the dark. Wild! Then I remembered that I was a new person, I was Dad's girl, and I didn't know when I'd be seeing Sandy again. Sandy. I hope she's not too upset. I hope she doesn't think it's her fault for being late.

I turned away from the body glow and flicked open a tabloid newspaper. There I was. My face, staring out at me. This time it was a holiday snap. I remembered the yellow T-shirt and the combat shorts. I remembered the place it was taken, an island near Sicily. There was a volcano in the background. Stromboli, that was it. It made me think of something to eat, something long and stringy with melted cheese on top. Henry had taken the photograph, and Mum had been standing behind him saying, "Smile, for goodness' sake, smile. Look happy for a change." And I did; for me, I looked quite happy. "The search continues for kidnapped daughter of TV personality Diane Murray," the caption said. "Eleven-year-old Holly . . ." "Eleven!" I said out loud. "I'm nearly fifteen!" I closed the newspaper quickly and went out of the shop. Dad had finished his call.

"That's done," he said. "I said I'll give them a ring in a couple of days and see if they've managed to save her, poor old girl. Can't bear the thought of losing her, but I've a feeling she's had it. You were practically born in her. . . . Ah, yes, we've got a story about that. Let's find this caff first."

He stopped an old man and asked him to point out the way to the transport café. "It'll take you about ten minutes," the old man said. "You young things!" Dad lifted his shoulders and grinned at me. "Takes me about half an hour, but there you are. Slow, slow, quick, quick, slow!" The old man did a kind of shuffling sidestep between us and then ambled off, humming to himself.

People seemed to be much nicer these days. I wondered if it was because we weren't in the city, where everyone's always rushing with no time to talk, or whether it was something to do with the way I was feeling. Or maybe it was Dad; he always had such a big, friendly smile when he talked to people. Maybe they were just bound to be friendly back to him. I decided I would always smile at people when I spoke to them and see if it made them friendly and jokey. I could try it out on Mr. Grummock, our chemistry teacher. Magic, if he smiled back! Real chemistry magic! I beamed at myself in a shopwindow. Only it wasn't me; it was someone dressed up to go trekking in the Himalayas. Or maybe to the Austrian Alps, in search of the ice man.

"Come on, Dilly Dawdler," Dad said.

"Okay, young thing. I'll race you!"

I streaked off ahead of Dad, and in no time at all he'd caught me up and was overtaking me. No way was I going to let him beat me. We went whooping down the High Street, scattering mothers with buggies and jumping over dog leads and I *won*! He called me back just as I was about to charge into the transport café.

"A man of my age should be allowed a bit of dignity," he panted. "Just hang on while I get my breath back." Then he sprinted past me and pulled open the door ahead of me. But the moral victory was mine, and he knew it.

It was hot and steamy inside the transport café. Truckers were eating breakfasts of eggs, beans, tomatoes, and chips and huge mugs of tea or coffee. Dad bought us a coffee each. "What are we doing here anyway?" I asked. "Not hitchhiking, Dad? You know what Mum would say!"

"Exactly! Now, I'm just going to say two things. Never, never do this on your own, Holly Starcross. Promise."

"I promise."

"As far as I can see, there's no other way of getting home from here. I'm going to get us as far as we can go in one lift, then ring Jody Tom to come and pick us up. You remember Jody Tom?"

"Don't think so."

"You must have been asleep. He was in my pop band. Matty Tom's dad. You don't remember Matty Tom? You used to kiss him in the hayricks."

"I never did."

"Yes, you did."

I blushed. "So? I was only five."

Dad nodded. "I'll see what I can fix up. By the way, I'm not asking for a free lift. I'll pay our way, or buy the chap a couple of meals for it." He stood up and then sat down again, grasping my hands. "See, Holly, it may be our only chance. The quicker we can get there, the better chance we have of a little more time together before your mother catches up with us. Because she will." He stood up again, scanning the room. "Matty Tom's a good-looking lad now. Helps in the stables. Great kid."

I watched Dad as he moved around the room, stopping to chat and joke with complete strangers, shaking their hands, big, friendly smile. It was as if he had always known them. And while I was watching him I was remembering about Matty Tom. Sliding down a hayrick, stuffing fistfuls of hay down each other's T-shirts, prickly, scratchy. "Stop it, Matty Tom. I'll tell your dad." And we were both giggling and sliding and snatching at each other's hair. "Give us a kiss then." So I did, a solemn little kiss that made us both giggle even more, and then Dad had come and carried us to the kitchen for milk and biscuits. And the trees were throwing shadowy arms around the house and shuffling their dry leaves like packs of playing cards.

Dad came back to the table with a plate of toasted tea cakes. He smiled ruefully. "I know we've only just had our breakfast, but I can't resist these."

"Dad!"

"Dripping with real butter. You don't have to have one. Lovely plump sultanas. Eh, smashing these are!"

"What happened to our lift then?"

"Fixed. We've got an Angel Gabriel called Stanley, and he's going to take us home. Home, Holly Starcross. What d'you think of that?"

I had a mouthful of hot tea cake, and the butter was dribbling down my chin. "Mmm." I was too happy to think of anything else to say. "Mmm."

"But he says he'll be about ten minutes because his tachometer says he's not had a long enough break yet, so I said that's fine, that's fine, because I was about to tell my girl a story anyway. You must be roasting in that fleece. Slip it off."

"I can't take my hat off, though," I said. "It's hiding my hair."

"Shall I tell you something?" Dad said, tweaking one of the pointy bits. "You look great in that hat. But you couldn't be more conspicuous if you tried."

"Conspicuous means kind of obvious?"

Dad nodded. I pulled off the cap, and my hair tumbled down.

"Smashing," he said. "Don't hide it."

"Dad!" I wasn't used to people saying nice things about me. I don't know what you're supposed to say back. "How about this story then?"

"Ah, yes. It's the story of the best day of my life. The first day of yours. You have that bit before I eat it. The day Holly Starcross came into the world. Ready?"

"It was Christmastime," I said.

"And you were due in mid-January. Your mother and I were traveling to her parents to spend Christmas with them. We loaded the car, that same car that's stuck in a garage, only it was a bit newer, and off we set. We'd been gone about an hour when it started to snow, and the further north we got, the heavier it fell. I wanted to turn back, but your mother was determined, we must go on, we must go on. She was quite hysterical about it. What I didn't know, and what she didn't know, was that she was actually very near to giving birth. You probably knew, but you won't remember. Well, a decision had to be made, and I think I made the wrong one. I decided to take a shortcut over the moors.

"Imagine the scene. Gray moors. Gray sky. Gray sheep. Nothing else for mile after mile. And the snowflakes falling thicker and faster around us. Your mother was sitting tense and tight and wordless, but that was her way sometimes. I just thought, She's mad with me for taking this shortcut. She's not going to speak to me again till we get to her parents. You know your mother. She never shouts. She just goes into a long silence, and that means trouble." He chuckled. "Are you like that, Holly Starcross?"

"Sometimes." I thought of the hours I spend in my room, too angry and upset to talk to anyone. "It helps to talk to Zed."

"You must tell me about this Zed sometime."

"I don't know any more, not really, not unless it's Aaron Hamilton."

"And do you really think it is Aaron Hamilton?"

I shook my head. I could feel that traitor flush creeping over my neck. "He wouldn't be interested in me. I'm too young."

"And you're a very pretty girl. Soon you'll have a great queue of lads knocking at the door for you."

My blush was all over my face now. No one, ever, had told me I was pretty. "Go on." I smiled. "It was snowing. . . ."

"It certainly was. And I took a sharp bend too quickly and plowed into a snowdrift. Try as I could, I couldn't back out. I told your mother she'd have to get out of the car. And I'll never in all my life forget how I felt when she said, 'I can't. The baby's coming.'

"I was twenty-seven years old. I know that sounds like an old man to you, but I can tell you I was no more than a lad. I was stuck in a snowdrift, and my wife was just about to have a baby! I didn't know whether to laugh or cry! I was dancing round in the snow, frightened and excited at the same time. I wrapped her up in my coat—my heron coat—and off I ran in my shirtsleeves, slipping and slithering and yelling. At last I came to a farmhouse. I battered on that door fit to break it down, and a deaf old woman came muttering and grumbling, and at last I got her to understand what was happening.

"Her son got out his tractor and trailer; he was as calm as a milk bottle. He coaxed your mother out of the car and lifted her down into the trailer as if it was something he had to do every day of his life, and I ran alongside, holding her hand and promising her we'd have her in hospital in no time.

"But you knew otherwise. You knew what life was all about, and your journey had already started. The waters had broken, if you know what that means. And the old woman at the farm knew how close you were to daylight. As soon as she saw your mother, she said, 'By, bairn's all but come. Get her inside.' We put her on the kitchen table. There's something women know about each other at times like this. I've birthed horses and ponies, and though it was my wife who was in labor and my child who was coming, I still stepped back and let the old woman take charge. All I could do was hold Diane's hand and wish I could take the pain for her.

"And then the wonderful thing happened. You came into the world. Head first, like a chestnut peeping from its shell, out you came, and you slithered into the old woman's arms like a slippery fish, my glistening mackerel baby. Eh? My miracle. You were born! You were perfect.

"The son had pulled my car out of the drift with his tractor, so I was able to phone for an ambulance to take you both to hospital. That was what Diane wanted. And when we left the house, the old woman was fast asleep by her fire, and I couldn't wake her up to say good-bye. I wanted to say thank you. Tiny words, for such big events.

"As I drove away from the farm, I noticed a holly tree by the gate, blazing with berries. It was as if it was shouting to the world, 'Look! Look! There's a baby! A baby's just been born!'"

"And that's how I got my name!"

"And next spring we set off again to visit your proud

grandparents, Grandma and Granddad Douglas. I suggested to your mother that we should go over the moors and visit the farm, so we could show you off to the old lady and thank her properly. But do you know, we couldn't find it. Searched and searched, drove up every lane and farm track, and not a trace of it. It was as if the whole place—the house, the son, the old woman, the holly tree—had never ever been."

· 19 ·

I came out of Dad's story, the story of me, as if I were in a trance. I couldn't make out where I was and why people were laughing and chattering to one another, banging plates onto tables, scraping chairs in a hot and steamy room. I couldn't make out why a big man with tattooed arms and a whiskery ginger chin was smiling down at me and why Dad was holding out his hand to him.

"Time for off, squire." The man grinned a smile of golden teeth.

"This is Stanley," Dad said. "He's going to take us home."

We followed Stanley out to a huge Weetabix carrier. The cab was so high off the ground that Dad had to lift me into it. It was decorated with family photographs and postcards of tropical fish. A nodding dog smelling of chemical flowers, the sharp smell of diesel and hot metal, and Stanley's smell of chips and sweat all mingled together. It was quite nice. I loved being so high up and looking down at all the traffic on the motorway. We overtook a car with a sunroof, and I could see the shiny pink of the driver's bald patch.

"I wouldn't normally give a lift to strangers. Have to be careful these days. But I saw you two when you walked in the caff, and I thought, That's nice, that is, a dad and his girl going around together."

Dad, for once, was absolutely silent. He picked up my *Man in the Ice* book and started leafing through it. Charlotte Church came on the radio, and I wondered what it must be like to be so famous and still be a child like me. I daydreamed for a bit about being discovered as a cellist. But how could I be a world-famous cellist if I couldn't practice? I made a promise to myself then that when I got home, I would tell Mum the truth, that I had a school cello and that I was having lessons, and I wouldn't ask her, I would *tell* her that I needed to have my own cello so I could practice every day at home. She would have to know how much it mattered to me. No more secrets.

It was brilliant then, looking out at the busy streets. I tried snatching stories about people as I passed them. A girl in the street was waving at someone unseen in an upstairs window. Perhaps it was her granny, who was bedridden, and every time the girl passed the house they waved to each other. Perhaps it was a secret meeting place with someone she wasn't allowed to meet, and she was signaling to say it was safe to come down now. A man kneeling in a garden. Perhaps he was praying for rain. Or burying his dog. Or trying to remember where he'd hidden his savings. A boy peering inside a letterbox. Had he just written to his girlfriend to say he never wanted to see her again, and now he'd changed his mind, and he was trying to get the letter back? Oh, too late, too late! Imagine her reading it next morning and weeping into her Weetabix. Or maybe he'd posted his glove instead of a letter. Or maybe he'd heard a voice inside the letterbox: "Help, help, get me out of here. . . ."

We arrived outside Manchester late afternoon. Stanley dropped us off, and we took a bus to the train station. I thought about our buses outside school: Sandy and I giggling and pink, dodging about, trying to catch a glimpse of Aaron on one of the top decks, kids pushing each other and messing about. I thought about running into our house and cuddling Zoe, and I could smell her and feel her soft breath on my cheek and the clasp of her sticky hands in my hair. Does she miss me? I thought about running upstairs with Panto lolloping behind and flinging my bag on my bed. Would there be any e-mail messages for me? Suddenly I was missing my mum again. I gave a little involuntary sob, and Dad turned to look at me.

"Too much?"

I nodded.

"Come here, Holly Starcross." He put his arm across my shoulder and I leaned against him and his smell was comforting and familiar from long ago.

When we got to the station, Dad sat me down in the restaurant and bought a pot of tea and two sticky Danish pastries. I hadn't said a word all this time. It was as if all the talking had dried up.

"You choose."

I shook my head, numb.

He cut the pastries in half. One had apples inside; the other had pecan nuts. He put half of each on each plate and pushed one toward me. "We'll ring your mother from here. I can put you on a train, and she can meet you at the other end. If that's what you really want, I'll do it. You'll be home by ten."

My throat was burning. I didn't know. I didn't know what I wanted.

"It was selfish of me. I shouldn't have done it this way."

I nodded again, picking at the apple pastry with my fingernail.

"I'll go and check out the train times. You sit here. I'll buy your ticket; then you can phone your mother. It's all right, Holly. It's all right."

I watched him go out of the café. A waitress came and swabbed at the table with a damp cloth, pushing our plates this way and that. I looked again, and there was no sign of my dad. I panicked. The crowds had swallowed him up. The waitress clattered his chair back under the table. I grabbed my rucksack and ran through the swing doors out onto the forecourt. Pigeons chuttered away from my feet. I darted up and down the station foyer, past the row of telephones, past the ticket booths, past the boutiques and the W. H. Smith shop. There was no sign of him anywhere. I wanted to howl like a lost kid in a supermarket, "Where's my daddy? I want my daddy."

Then I saw him in front of the departures monitor, craning his head, screwing up his eyes to read it because he'd sat on his reading glasses. Oh, Dad, oh, Dad! I ran straight to him, colliding with a woman who was dragging two tartan suitcases on roller wheels. Sorry, sorry. "Dad!" I reached him at last. "I don't want to go home yet. I want to come with you."

"Sure? Sure?" His face was like a rosy apple with smiles. He kissed my forehead quickly and took my hand. Together we went to the ticket booth. "Two for Noedale," Dad said. "One adult, one child." Noedale. A flower of happiness opened up inside me. I was really going home.

Dad gave me my ticket. "Here you are. You're in charge of this now. The train leaves in forty minutes, and if you happen to be on it, I'll be delighted."

"I will be!" I promised. "I won't change my mind again. Noedale!" I was jumping up and down on my toes with excitement. I just couldn't help it.

"And I believe I left you in charge of two delicious cakes and a pot of tea?"

"I'm famished!" I shouted. We ran back to the café, shouting, "Pecan's best! No, apple's best!" at each other. The waitress was just clearing them onto her tray. "Wait! They're ours!" I shouted from the doorway.

She put them back with a bored sigh. "Lucky for you I recognized your hat. People are always coming in here pinching other people's food."

"I knew this hat would come in useful!" I told Dad, triumphant. But part of me was fluttering nervously. I knew there was something I had to do before we left.

This time Dad came to the phone booth with me. He was smiling encouragement. I tried to pretend I was calm about it, but my hands wouldn't stop shaking. Don't make a fuss. Please, please don't make a fuss. Mum answered the phone straightaway.

"Mum."

"Holly? Is that Holly? For God's sake, where are you?"

"I'm at the station."

"I can tell that! Which station? Are you coming home?"

I swallowed hard. "No. Not yet."

"What are you doing?" Mum's voice was shrill and loud. "Who are you with? Is it your father, Holly?"

I couldn't answer that. "I'm fine, Mum. Really, truly, I'm fine. I just rang to tell you that."

"Who are you with? What on earth do you think you're doing?"

I put my hand over the receiver. I couldn't bear to listen to her. Then I broke into her questions. "Mum, listen, please listen. I promise I'm well. I promise I'll be home soon."

"When? Don't you know I'm worried sick about you?"

My money was running out. Dad held out another coin.

"How's Zoe?"

"Zoe's all right. For God's sake, child, who are you with?"

Counting down. Ten, nine, eight . . . "Stop worrying," I shouted down the receiver, drowning out her voice again. "I'll phone again soon." Silence, Mum's voice snatched away. I put the receiver on its hook and gave Dad his coin back. "The things I do for you!" I tried to smile, but I don't think it came out right. I didn't feel like smiling. We walked to our platform. My ticket was a crumpled ball in the palm of my hand.

"Another forty minutes on the train," Dad said. "And it'll still be light when we arrive. I could phone Jody and ask him to meet us, but he'll be busy with the milking. Can you face a half-hour walk? Then we'll be there. We'll be home."

I could hardly believe I was actually on the last stage of the journey. I was a little afraid in case I didn't like the house when we got there. I didn't really know what I was going to find. I kept thinking about our warm, comfortable house in the leafy suburbs and all the city lights coming on by now, the cars nosing away from the center to the suburbs and the motorway, people going to their homes. I thought of the twins curled up on the settee eating jam sandwiches, teasing Panto. And I thought of Zoe.

"Want another story?" Dad asked when we were on the train. I shook my head. The people he had told me about swam around like ghost fish in a slow, silent dance of their own, as if they were listening to their own music: Maggie with her billowing skirt and her eyes closed shut, dancing dreamily to music only she could hear. I thought about the boy trudging up the mountain with a poppy red scarf for his sweetheart. What if his mother had never found him? What if he had died up there in his huddle of rocks? Dad would never have been born; I would never have been born. A world without me—imagine! I must have laughed out loud. Dad was flicking through the photographs in my *Man in the Ice* book. He looked up and smiled at me, but I shook my head. I didn't want to share it. The train rocked out of the station. I thought again of Jake setting out on his search for Zosia, across strange countries, just pulled by his love for her. What if he had never found her? What if he had given up his search or fallen in love with somebody else? What if they had stayed in Austria, and Dad and Maggie had been born, but who would Dad have married? Not Mum. I thought of Dad struggling with his music. What if his band had won and he'd become a famous rock star? What if he'd married a rich American girl? . . . There wouldn't have been me . . . not me as I am now. Not Holly Starcross, named after a tree in the snow in a farmyard that's disappeared. And if Mum hadn't left Dad and gone on to live with Henry, there would have been no Zoe.

"Dad." I leaned forward and pressed the book down. "Can I tell you a story?"

"About?"

"My sister . . ."

Three old ladies with identical glasses and identical shoes nodded and smiled on the seats opposite us. The middle one kept closing her eyes and dropping her head forward, and the other two closed their shoulders up to hers without looking at her and without saying anything, propping her up.

Dad nodded.

"Mum and Henry are . . . well, they're kind of beautiful." I wrinkled my nose because it was embarrassing to say it, but it was true. "They're like film stars. And they've got twins, a boy and a girl, and they're beautiful, too."

"Perfect family."

"When I was little, I was jealous of the twins. They got so much attention. Mum said I wasn't a bit like them. She said I was a cuckoo in the nest."

Dad sighed.

"But I had to look after them a lot, even though I was only little. Then Mum went into hospital to have another baby. I wrote to you again to come and take me away, but you didn't come."

"I never got the letter, Holly."

"I never sent it. It's in my shoebox along with all the others." And if I had known where to send it to, if I had dared ask my mother, what would have happened? She might not have wanted me anymore.

"So." Dad closed the book. I noticed he was on the chapter about the last journey of the ice man, before the snows of winter covered him up for five thousand years. I wondered if the ice man would have been thinking about his family when he was walking away from them into the mountains. "And the baby was Zoe," Dad prompted.

"It's funny . . . I didn't even want to look at the twins when they were born, but I couldn't wait to see the new baby girl. Henry took me in to see her. Before we went, he bought me a little baby doll of my own, and I went in carrying it wrapped up in a shawl that Grandma Douglas had given me. But Mummy . . . Mum wasn't holding her baby. She was crying. She told

Henry that she didn't want her baby. She cried and cried for weeks. She came home with the baby, and she wouldn't hold her or look at her. I used to sit and nurse her for hours. Mum said she wasn't beautiful; she said there was something wrong with her. We thought the baby was going to die and Mum didn't care. She didn't want the baby. She let me look after her all the time. We had a nurse who came every day, and she said if I hadn't loved Zoe so much, she mightn't have lived. She had to go to hospital. Mum had to stay with her all the time, and they let me stay, too."

"What was the matter with Zoe?"

"She had weak lungs, but she's better now. She's got Down's syndrome. She's really pretty. Not beautiful like Lisa and Julian, but pink-and-golden pretty. She laughs a lot when she's happy, and when she's sad, she just cries and cries. Mum says I'm the only one who can cheer her up when she's like that."

"You're too young to have that responsibility."

"That's what Henry says."

I leaned back. I had wanted to tell Dad about Zoe, about how special she was, that I worried about her all the time.

"So what are you thinking, Holly?"

It was hard. So hard. I felt as if I was handling ideas that were so fragile they might slip away as soon as I tried to touch them, like ice crystals. I used to catch flakes of snow and try to run home with them before they melted, they were so beautiful. "I've been thinking about Grandpa Jake and Nana Zosia and Granddad and Grandma Douglas, and how if it wasn't for them, I wouldn't exist. Or you and Mum, if it wasn't for you. And I know I look like you, but I look a bit like Grandma Douglas, too—"

"The eyes."

"Or something. And I play cello, and that's like Nana Zosia, and I can't make good pastry because my hands are too warm like Mum's, and I've got little toes like her sister, and there're all those sorts of things."

"Go on."

"But Henry is nothing to do with me, not really, yet he's taught me how to play chess and backgammon and things, and I can do French better than anyone else in our class because he talks to me in French sometimes."

"Go on. . . ."

"And Zoe . . . I was really spiteful and jealous and horrible about the twins, but I'm not like that with Zoe. When I'm with her, I just want to smile and be gentle and loving. That's what she does to me." I gazed out the window. Dad was smiling. I didn't know he'd understood what I was trying to say. I wasn't sure I understood it myself. We were drawing out of the long darkness of a tunnel. The track was lined with the gray-green ghosts of twilight trees, and their branches were black scribbles as if they were cracks in the gray sky. The hills were like the long spines of sleeping dinosaurs. There were buildings dotted about, their lights like glowing eyes. My heart gave slow, steady turns. I recognized it. I was quite sure I recognized it. I pressed my face against the glass.

"We're here, aren't we?" I said, and Dad nodded and handed me my rucksack.

"We're here."

· 20 ·

No one else got off. I was glad. The train rolled away, and we were alone on Noedale station.

"I think it's just the same," I said. My voice sounded tiny and strange with all that wide echoey air around me.

"Nearly. Streetlights on the platform. They're new. A bus shelter for Sunday hikers. A huge car park. All a bit urban for the likes of me. But down our end, nothing's changed. Okay to walk?"

I wanted to savor this last bit. I wanted to get used to it slowly, like coming out of a dream.

The evening was settling around us. I recognized the smell of the lane. I wanted to run and shout along it as if I were five years old again. Instead I walked as quietly as I could, listening to all the whisperings around me, and it was as if they were saying, "Holly Starcross is coming home." Sheep coughed and baaed to one another.

When we came to the railway bridge, a badger scuttled through a hole in the hawthorn hedge and shimmied out of sight. We passed the gate of the farm where Demon used to live and the barn where Dad and his band used to practice. We walked over a stone bridge and looked down at the peaty brown water. The last of the leaves rustled in the trees over our heads, whispers and chuckles and long-ago secrets. An owl with quiet wings drifted away, and then we heard it call, long and shivery, from the plantation on the far hillside.

"Old tawny," Dad said. "They've all come out to greet you tonight."

I couldn't trust myself to speak, I was so excited. We came to a group of cottages, and I immediately remembered the names of the people who lived there. Ray, the artist who used to take me for walks and find wildflowers to paint. Steffie and Ken, who let me throw kibbled corn for their hens in the mornings and crouch down to feel for eggs in the straw. I could feel them warm in my hands. I could hear again the chuttering and crooning of the sleepy hens at night.

And there was the farm. There was a huddle of old barns, where I used to play with Matty, the stables where the horses were kept, and, just past them, there was a cottage with its doorway lantern shining through a tangle of honeysuckle branches.

"That's it! That's our house!"

I started to run. I could easily reach the chain that was looped round the gatepost. I used to have to climb up to open it. I ran up the path and pushed open the front door, and there was the room, and it was just as if I'd never never left it: the threadbare sofa in front of the fire, the piles of books, the cats stretching themselves.

And there was little Nana Zosia, leaning forward in her chair and pushing herself out of it to stand up. She hugged me to her as if I were a little child again.

"My darling Holly. My darling little Holly Starcross. I've waited here since your father went looking for you. Oh, I knew he'd find you. I knew he'd bring you home! Look at you! My big girl! Welcome home!"

Nothing had changed. I walked around the house touching things and naming them: the flowered plate, the cane chair, the painting of a barn with a blue door, the lamp with the brass stand, the bent shovel on the hearth. Nana never took her eyes off me as I walked around. She kept clapping her hands and laughing and crying and saying how tall I'd grown and how pretty I was, and just look at my hair, like a horse's mane! She hummed her deep old sad songs and stretched her bent fingers just as I had remembered her doing. She asked me about the cello and said I was lucky to have music in me; it would fill my life with wonderful sounds.

"Nana," I said, "how do you know I play the cello?"

And she said, "I always knew you would play the cello."

I put that away in my head to think about. "Where's Grandpa Jake?"

Nana put her fingers to her lips. "Asleep. Such a surprise he'll have tomorrow! I expect you're starving, aren't you? Do you still like baked spuds?"

I went up to my bedroom at last. My room, with a beam that was a whole tree stretching from one end of it to the other, and walls that bulged with age, and pictures that had been there when my great-grandmother was a child. I put on the sprigged nightie that Nana had brought for me and that smelled of lavender, and I lay in bed listening to the rush of the stream and the distant barking of the fox, and I thought, There's nowhere else in the world I would rather be. I'm truly home.

· 21 ·

I woke up next morning to the unfamiliar sound of a farmer driving sheep down the lane under my window. Their hooves pattered like rain as they hurried along. I lay looking up at the crazed ceiling and listening to a relentless chanting of birdsong, and then, suddenly, I remembered where I was. I jumped out of bed and pulled back the curtain. Autumn leaves lay scattered across the grass like golden mushrooms. I could see Dad in the farmyard. He was leaning on the wall, watching the sheep piling into their pen. The dog was crouched in the lane, absolutely fixed on them, bossy as a teacher. Dad said something to Jody Tom, who put his hand across his eyes and looked up toward my bedroom window.

"Welcome home, Holly Starcross!" he called. I was shy, but I waved back. I wondered if he still minded about the time I'd slid down his hayloft and spilled hay all across the barn floor.

When I went downstairs, the fire was lit, and there were eggs and bread on the table for me. I was too excited to eat. I ran down to the stables, skipping around the muddy bits that the sheep had churned up. Dad was just starting to sweep out, lifting up great wads of damp hay and horse muck and tipping them into a wheelbarrow. He nodded toward the end stable. I hesitated. I didn't know if I was ready to see Rosa yet. I was frightened of her, after all this time. He was watching me. I didn't dare tell him how I felt. It didn't make sense. I went in quietly. Rosa was eating. She swung her head around to look at me, and I stood still, taking in the darkness and the rich, dusty smell. She rolled her eyes and flattened her ears. I didn't dare touch her. I sensed Dad standing behind me.

"Want to ride her?"

I shook my head. I didn't know how to ride anymore. But I didn't want to let Dad down.

"Take your time," he said, sensing me. "There's no rush."

He went back outside, whistling. I heard him sweeping again. I was used to the darkness now, and the smell, and the way Rosa shifted her heavy hooves. I took a slow step forward. Rosa swung her long head round again and stamped, and I backed out quickly. No point getting trampled on my first day home, I was thinking, shutting the door. Then I realized there was someone watching me. It was a farm boy. He turned away when I looked at him and whistled to the dog.

I went to climb the stone stile, and when I swung back around, the boy was standing with his hands on his hips, watching me again.

"All right?" he said.

"Yeah. Hi."

"You're Holly. I remember you."

I felt myself going red. Oh no, I thought, this can't be Matty! I remembered what Dad had said about him, that he'd turned into a nice-looking lad. Oh, glory, and I used to play with him every day, and now look how tall he was, and how piercing blue his eyes were, and how his hair fell about his face. I turned and ran back to the house and didn't give him another look. But I thought about him, all right, and wondered if he was thinking about me. I helped myself to breakfast and then went slowly around each of the rooms, and it was like running back an old video and remembering the story as it unfolded. I picked up jugs and plates and books and pictures, and they carried voices inside them from when I was a little girl and it was Mummy and Daddy and nothing was going wrong.

"Good morning, Holly," came a voice behind me, and I dropped the carved owl I was holding. It didn't break but rolled unsteadily on its rounded back.

"Did you sleep well?" Nana Zosia asked me. She walked slowly and painfully toward me and hugged me. We were the same height; in fact, if you counted my hair, I was a few centimeters taller.

"You don't live here, do you, Nana? I remember your cottage at Vale End. I was going to try to find it this morning and surprise you."

"Oh, we had to sell that two or three years ago. Your grandpa took bad, couldn't work anymore. And I'm next to useless with perishing arthritis. No, we sold up and moved back here, where we'd always lived, where your grandfather was born. He's upstairs, if you want to see him. Go on, take his brekkie tray up. He'd like that."

I remembered a man with dark curly hair and a deep voice, a strong, quiet man who had a way with horses that was like a magic spell. And as I was going upstairs with the tray of cornflakes and tea, I thought about the boy who had been carried over the moors on his mother's back and the man who had been so wild with love for his Zosia that he had wandered around the world looking for her. They were all like different pieces of the same jigsaw.

I pushed open the door and went in. The bedroom was dark because the curtains were still closed. I could just make out the bed with its iron bars and a still heap inside it. Nana followed behind me. "Now, Jake, sit up and smile because I've brought the child to see you."

And this breathy whisper came from somewhere inside the bedspread. "Is it her? Has she come?"

Nana pushed me forward. "He's been hanging on for you."

She pulled back the curtains, and the shape in the bed moved slightly, covering his eyes with a long, thin hand. I set the tray on the table by the bed. I wanted to turn away and run outside, but the hand reached over and caught mine and pressed it. I sat on the edge of the bed. A pale face turned to look at me. His hair was chalky white and straggly on the pillow. How could he have changed so much?

"Little Holly Heartthrob," he mumbled. It made me smile, and the pale, gaunt face softened as though the sun had come out. He pressed my hand to his lips. "Are you all right, Holly?"

"I am, Grandpa."

"You look all right. Can you whistle yet?"

"I can." I demonstrated. The only tune I could think of was "Rudolph the Red-Nosed Reindeer." He joined in, breathy and earnest, tapping out the rhythm on my hand with his bony fingers. It seemed important to get to the end of the tune without smiling.

"Not bad," he said when we'd finished. He was exhausted.

Nana patted his cheek, really gently, as if she were tidying up his skin and putting it back in place.

"I'll be up and about tomorrow," he said. It was hard to hear him. "I'll tek you up on top. See the heather."

"Heather's gone," Nana said gently. "Weeks ago."

"Aye." He sighed. "Reckon it has." He turned his face away.

"I've brought you some breakfast, Grandpa. I'll read to you after if you like."

"Used to tek you tobogganing up there. Down the peat lanes. Eh? Screamed like a magpie tha did, wi' the fun out it. Cheeks like apples, hair like a hawthorn hedge."

Nana's eyes were bright. "She's offered to sit and read to you."

"I've got a library book," I said. "It's about the man who was discovered in the ice."

Nana drew in her breath. "Hoetzi, the ice man," she said.

"Guess how old he is?"

"You tell me."

"Five thousand years old!"

"Wey, he's even older'n me!" Grandpa chuckled.

"There's a tree," said Nana, "that's five and a half thousand years old and still living! Imagine! It was an old tree when Hoetzi, the ice man, was a boy. Imagine what it's seen!" Her voice was misty with wonder. "It's called the Methuselah tree." She stood up and went over to the door. "You look after my Methuselah for a bit," she said. "Make sure he gets some breakfast down him."

I spent the morning with Grandpa, chatting to him and reading to him. I suddenly realized that the sound of his breathing had changed and that he had fallen asleep. He looked peaceful. I knew that he was very ill. Nobody could be so pale and thin and weak unless he was very ill. I was afraid. What if he died while I was in the room on my own with him? Then I thought, But it wouldn't be much different from now, would it? He would just be asleep, and then the sleep would be too deep for him to come out of. The door opened quietly, and Dad came in and stood by me, looking down at Grandpa Jake, not saying anything. And then he just bent down and kissed his forehead, as if Grandpa were a little boy and Dad were his father.

"I brought you home in time," Dad said. "He wanted to see his little Holly Heartthrob again."

That afternoon Nana stayed up in the room with Grandpa Jake while Dad and I went for a walk. We went over the fields to the village to buy a few things from the post office store. We kept meeting people, and Dad would stop and chat to them, and then he'd say, "Know who this is, don't you?" And his voice would be swelling with pride. "It's Holly, come back home."

The response would always be the same. "Holly Starcross! Haven't you grown!" Why do adults always say that, as if it were a surprise? It would be much more surprising if I was still the same height as I was eight years ago, that's for sure.

We paused outside the village school. The windows were covered with pictures of autumn leaves and squirrels.

"They'll be taking them down soon," I said. "Then it'll be snowflakes and Father Christmas and angels." We could hear Mrs. Tym's voice. She was teaching the children a song, and their little piping voices straggled after hers like lambs bleating behind a ewe.

"Mrs. Tym would love to see you," Dad said. "Just imagine her face if you walked into the classroom now."

"No," I said firmly. "No, no, no."

"I take it you don't like the idea."

"I'd die of embarrassment. I already feel as if I'm some sort of freak because I happen to be twice as big as I was eight years ago."

I lingered outside the post office store while Dad did the shopping. The window was just as it had always been, a jumble of bottles of sweets, walking guides, dog biscuits, and mugs with pictures of Noedale printed on them. There was a machine of colored sweet balls and trinkets by the door and a notice board with adverts for holiday cottages, dog training, and chimney vacs. Nobody spoke to me while I was there. Nobody even noticed me without Dad exhibiting me. The chanting from the school stopped, the door opened, and the children burst into the yard, squealing like parrots. I turned away quickly. "Let me be invisible," I prayed. I pulled my fleece hat firmly over my hair, and kept my back to the school. Another day.

When we arrived back at the cottage, Nana beckoned mysteriously to Dad, and he followed her into the living room. I was so frightened that she was going to tell him something about Grandpa that I followed, not hiding, but standing in the doorway where she couldn't see me but Dad could.

"The police have just been," she told him.

Dad groaned. "Already!"

"I told them you weren't here. It was not a lie, but it was not the truth. I told them I was looking after a sick husband, and I did not want to alarm him. I asked them to go away, and they did."

"I've told half the village she's here."

"Of course you have. You're a fool. You'll lose her again."

I turned back to the kitchen and made myself busy unloading the shopping. I wondered what I would do if the police suddenly burst in and dragged me away to my mother. I took two apples out of the fruit bowl and tossed them from one hand to the other, up and up, higher and higher and faster and faster. I didn't know I was doing it till Dad came behind me and caught one.

"Can you walk on stilts, too?" he asked.

"Apparently," I told him. "Remember, I'm the tallest six-year-old in Noedale." We both laughed, as if he hadn't had that conversation with Nana, as if I hadn't overheard it. We were going to pretend it had never happened.

In the evening Auntie Maggie came around. She

came in full of energy and cold fresh air and laughter, and she kissed me and told me how tall I'd grown, which made Dad wink at me, and then she just kind of switched off and sat quiet and wrapped up in herself, staring at me and smiling from time to time as if she couldn't think of anything else to say. After a bit she asked me if I wanted to go and sit with Grandpa with her. I watched how gently she stroked his hand, as if he were a little sleeping animal. She told me her husband was at home looking after the boys. Did I know she had two little boys? I shook my head. I didn't know anything about her except that long ago she had loved Demon and he had been killed. Did she dream about him? I wondered. Did it still hurt to think about him? I didn't dare ask her in case it made her cry or in case she thought it was none of my business. But you are my auntie, and we're made of the same stuff. We come from the same star.

"Have you still got that red dress?" I asked her, and she gave me a strange, puzzled look.

Grandpa slept the whole time. I gazed around the room that was his and Nana's. There was an old chest of drawers and a big dark wardrobe and a rickety table, and this iron bed that made me think of *Charlie and the Chocolate Factory* and the two sets of grandparents sleeping at either end. And there was a computer. That was quite amazing. I went and sat in front of it and switched it on out of habit.

"Is this Grandpa's?" I asked.

"No," Auntie Maggie said. "It's your nana's. She spends hours e-mailing people. Now she doesn't get out and about, it's her lifeline. She's even got her own Web site."

I swiveled around on the embroidered chair. My head was rocking. "What kind of Web site?" I asked.

It was Grandpa who answered, drowsy with sleep. "Music, music, music," he sang, without opening his eyes, and then fell asleep again.

But something was beginning to click into place. How did Dad find me? Why did he come to my school? I searched in my head for the pieces of the pattern. A long time ago I had e-mailed the musicbox Web site and I had said, "I am nearly fourteen years old, and I go to Hazelwood School." I'm sure that's what I wrote. And ever since then I had been e-mailing Zed and hoping against hope that he was Aaron Hamilton and that he would talk to me in school. But he hadn't. It wasn't Aaron at all. Of course it wasn't. But could Zed possibly be my own grandmother?

Downstairs, when we were washing up the supper dishes, I said casually, "Zed for Zosia." Nana said nothing. Just chuckled. Just wiped the plates with her poor twisted hands and chuckled.

Later she said she had something for me in the back room. She held my hand when we went in. The curtains were closed, and it was dark, and it smelled fusty as if no one went in there anymore. She put the light on, and there in the corner was a cello in a brown case. "Take it out," she said eagerly. Her eyes were as bright as rain. Dad came into the room and just stood in the doorway, his hands in his pockets. I took out the cello and stroked it. I loved the shiny feel of the wood and the curve of its body. There was a yellow polishing cloth inside the case, and I rubbed the wood with it, making its deep brown gleam like chestnut fire.

"Will you tune it?" Nana said.

I could do that easily. I sat on one of the dining chairs and leaned the cello against myself. Its voice spoke in the room, making the furniture tremble.

"Ah!" Nana said. "Such a sound! You have a good ear, Holly. The tuning is perfect. Now"—she clasped her hands like a little girl, reminding me of Lisa when she wants something special—"play for me."

My cheeks were flaming. "Nana," I said, "I'm not even in the orchestra."

"Why not?" she asked. "You love playing. You told me many times."

Zed for Zosia.

"Play," Nana said.

And I did. I was nervous, but there was one piece that I knew very well and that I loved playing. Nobody but my teacher had ever heard me play it. Now I played it for Nana and Dad, and it was like giving them a gift, and the music told them about how much I had longed to come home again. It said more than any words could have said. When I finished playing, I sat with my eyes closed, and there was a long silence in the room, holding the last note, and it drifted away like a slow breath.

Then Nana said, "You can play, Holly Starcross."

Dad came over and kissed me. "Thank you, little one," he said.

"How can you bear it, not to be able to play any-more?" I asked Nana. I couldn't help saying it.

"I couldn't bear it. It broke my heart. The day I packed my cello away and knew I would never play it again was the worst day of my life. And that's when I thought of setting up the musicbox Web site on the Internet, to encourage children to play. I took an e-mail address: Zed at brainwave. It helped me, writing to children who loved music. Then a child called Holly started writing to me, and I found we could talk about all kinds of things, not just music."

Dad laughed. "You see, Holly, you think I'm an old dinosaur for not having a mobile phone or a TV or anything like that, and my mother here has been shooting messages into space for years! And one day she asked you your name."

My name? It's Holly Starcross. I remembered typing that. I think that was when my search for my self began.

Dad was still talking. I pulled myself back into the present. "And we've been hanging on to every word you've written since then! Just in case it *was* you. It had to be you, but we hardly dared hope, did we, Mum?"

"I knew it was my Holly," she said. "Her messages just reached out to me. And then we looked back to your very first e-mail and found you had actually named your school. Hazelwood School. There aren't many of those. So your father set off to find you. Oh, how I started singing again that day!" Nana clapped her hands together. "I thought I might have found my grandchild, and there she was, playing cello, as if she were the ghost of myself. I hardly dared believe it. It wasn't luck; it wasn't magic. It was meant to be."

I couldn't look at Dad. He'd known all the time who Zed was, and he'd let me pour out my soppy little heart to him about Aaron Hamilton. "I wish you'd told me," I said.

"You mean you wish you hadn't told me about Aaron Hamilton." He grinned.

I threw the polishing cloth at him.

"It doesn't matter who you thought Zed was," said Nana. "It brought you home again."

I put the cello away carefully. I was still reeling back all those e-mail messages. I had never really believed I was talking to Aaron Hamilton. I had thought I was talking to a stranger, because no one else wanted to listen to me. I stroked the cello's polished wood and closed down the lid.

"I'm going to teach you everything I know," my little nana said. "This is your cello now."

All night I heard the deep and lovely voice of the cello singing in my head. My cello. But I heard something else, too. It was the telephone. The first time it rang, Dad answered it. I could hear his voice raised and angry. Then he put the phone down. After that it rang many times, but nobody answered it. The house was holding its breath, waiting for the phone to ring again. It went on and on, like somebody crying all on her own, wanting to be comforted.

· 22 ·

Dad woke me very early next morning. The sky outside was hardly light.

"It's going to be a terrific morning," he said. "How about coming for a ride?'

"Now?" I was confused, seeing him standing there in the half-light, as if he were one of the shadows in my dream and had just stepped out of it. I couldn't even see his face properly. Then he switched on my bedside light and became Dad again.

"I don't know," I said. "I haven't ridden for years. I don't know how to do it."

"You'll be fine. It'll be lovely. We'll be up on the tops to watch the dawn coming up. I want you to see it."

I struggled to pull myself out of my dream. Dancing shadows closed around me, as if they wanted to hold me.

"I'll be packing some stuff while you're getting dressed. I've borrowed some old riding clothes for you from Matty. We'll have a picnic breakfast."

He ran downstairs, and I could hear him whistling in the kitchen. Still half asleep, I scrambled into Matty's clothes and splashed my face with cold water. Dad was waiting outside for me when I came down. He was right. It was a fantastic morning already. There had been an overnight frost, and the grass and trees sparkled as if they'd had stars hanging from them. The sky was bruised with violet light. Dad led Skipper out and started harnessing him.

"Get Rosa," he said.

I went nervously into her stall. She whinnied at me, tossing her head, sensing that I was uneasy.

"It's all right, Rosa. We'll be all right." I stood very still, calming her, calming myself. Then I went up to her and stroked her. I could feel her tension draining away with mine. I put my head against her neck. "Lovely Rosa. Remember me?"

I led her into the yard. Dad had brought the tack, and I brushed her down quickly and saddled her up myself. Dad slipped the bridle over her head. She stood patiently, blowing white ghosts from her nostrils, anticipating the ride. Dad checked the girth and handed me a hat. He fastened the strap under my chin as if I were six years old again.

"Ready when you are."

"Ready." I swung myself up, easily, lightly, onto Rosa's back. She felt so good. Instinctively I tightened my thighs against her and felt her firm body rolling steadily under me as we walked out of the farmyard into the lane. I felt great. I felt fantastic. A sun that was as red as blood peered up behind the horizon of the hills. We kicked the horses into a trot. I was so easy and comfortable on Rosa that I felt as if there had never been a time when I hadn't been riding her.

We turned up a stony track. Jagger's Clough. I remembered it. I remembered the brambles where Matty and I used to pick blackberries, staining our fingers purple like bruises. I remembered the musty smell of Himalayan balsam, tall purple flowers that I used to sprig my hair with. Now the beech and sycamore leaves were spinning over my head, gold and tawny and scarlet, and the sunlight was trickling through and dabbling yellow lights on the grass like a painter. If anyone ever wants to ask me what was the best hour of my life, it was then. But before the day was over, everything had gone wrong, and I thought I would never be happy again.

From the top of the hill we could see four valleys.

"This is my forgotten planet," Dad said. "I used to come here when I was a young man courting."

"Courting!" I giggled. "Was it with Mum?" I couldn't imagine her using an old-fashioned word like that. But I couldn't imagine her riding a horse or even climbing up such a steep track, hot and red-faced and breathless. Mum was a city person in beautiful city clothes, city shoes, a city hairstyle.

"No. This was before your mother. This is my first girl I'm talking about. Julia. I thought it was a lovely name. Oh, I thought about her every minute of every day. I just about managed to bring her into every conversation I had; I wanted to talk about her all the time. We used to come up here and think we owned it all, everything we could see. I thought the end of the world had come when she jilted me. I was only seventeen, and I thought I'd never be happy again."

"Did you have other girlfriends?"

"After Julia? Not the same. Nothing was the same till I met your mother. Oh, I went out with girls. But, you can't help it, you can't force yourself to be in love. It just happens. Or it doesn't."

"How do you know when it's happened?"

"Eh? You'll find out. One day soon."

I felt embarrassed and kind of pushed out, as if being in love were like belonging to a club and you had to know the password to get in. Girls in school said they were in love, but they were only the same age as I was. I talked about being in love with Aaron Hamilton. Most of the time I was quite sure I was in love with him. I blushed at the sound of his name; I went weak and hot every time I caught sight of him. But could you really be in love with someone who's never even spoken to you? And was being in love the same as loving someone? It was all a vast mystery, a grown-up secret. But soon, Dad said, I would probably find out soon.

"Anyway, I thought I'd never love anyone again, and then one day I met your mother. It was love at first sight! I felt as if I were sixteen again, but I was a fair bit older than that!"

"Was she like Julia?"

"Nothing like. Julia was a country girl; in fact, you know her. She runs the post office. If you'd come in with me yesterday morning, you'd have seen her again. No, your mother was refined, elegant, beautiful. Far too good for me. But she'd had enough of the bright lights. I could see how bruised she was by that glossy world she lived in. I think she wanted to be somewhere quiet and out of the limelight. She needed protecting, and I wanted to do that for her, and I think she thought I was the only one who could. For a time. I think she loved me, for a bit."

I didn't dare say anything. I leaned forward and patted Rosa's neck, and she twitched her ears knowingly. I kept my eyes on a kestrel that was hovering just near us, as still as a breath.

"We got married six months later, and I think she regretted it from the very first day. A house in the country, miles from anywhere. She thought it was a dream. Look at the valley now, bathed in sunlight. Your heart goes out to it. It looks the most beautiful place on God's earth. It is. But it's like falling in love and falling out again to some folks. The reality was so different from the dream to her. In a few weeks the hills will disappear in mist, the rain will lash across the fields, the wind will howl night and day. The lanes will be running like rivers, and all the tracks will be kneedeep in mud. That's the reality your mother saw in the end, and she hated it."

The kestrel suddenly dropped like a stone and then swooped away across the valley. I wondered if it had caught anything. I don't know if Dad was actually aware of me just then. No one had ever talked to me like this before.

"And she saw me for what I really was." Dad went on, relentlessly. "A man with no ambition, a man who loved being outside whatever the weather, happier with animals than with people, happy to be here for the rest of his life. She wanted me to move to the city. How could I? She stuck it for seven years, and that was pretty wonderful when you think about it. She used to go away a lot. I thought she just needed a break; I never asked her about it. But after a bit I knew, deep down, that she was being courted by other men. I never thought she'd run away with one of them. I almost didn't mind what she did as long as I could stay here with my little girl. But she had to take you."

I thought of all the things Mum had said against Dad when I'd asked her about him. How he didn't care what she wanted. How he never listened to her when she begged him to move to somewhere more civilized.

"Hungry?" Dad asked.

"Starving. I could eat a horse—whoops, sorry, Rosa, didn't mean it."

We were suddenly very light and laughing with each other. Everything was silly, sitting on slopy boulders, cheese and pickle sandwiches for breakfast, Rosa and Skipper tugging at the grass under our feet, and the sheep nuzzling around us like beggars. One huge ewe climbed right across me and sat on me, trying to get at my sandwich. Dad had to roll her off. We toasted the golden morning with coffee from the flask.

After breakfast we cantered along the ridge, Dad's forgotten planet.

"It's fantastic up here," I said. "We can see the whole valley. Your house."

"Our house," Dad said.

It was tucked in behind a copse, tiny as a matchbox from here, a little gray heart of a house. I watched a white dot rolling like a bead along the thread of the lane. It turned right by Demon's farm and rolled slowly down toward our sheds.

"We've got a visitor," I said, and I knew Dad had seen it, too, but he turned away and looked down across the other valley, clicking his tongue softly behind his teeth.

"We don't have to go down yet. We could go on now. We've eaten, we're fine. Beautiful places I want to take you to. Vincent lives over there, in that other valley. We could ride there. We could stay at his place tonight, stable the horses, ride on tomorrow—show you the reservoir, pinewoods, see red squirrels there, so much to show you, Holly." He was already trotting on. His voice was breaking up.

Dad. Poor Dad. I knew what he was trying to tell me. I could hear it in his voice. I had heard it when we were eating our picnic breakfast, inside his laughter and jokes. I looked down again at the white bead. It had stopped in front of the gray, beating heart of the house.

"Dad, we have to go down." I felt older than he was. Much older. He was the child, bewildered and upset and running away. "We have to go home sometime."

I turned Rosa back the way we had come. Dad had stopped. We were waiting for each other.

"What are you going to do?" he called.

"I don't know." That was the truth. There was only one thing that I was sure of. The running was over. I kicked Rosa on. We jogged down the track, down and down the twisting zigzag path that wound through the larch copse to the cluster of cottages, the low barns and the shedding sycamores, the gray cottage, and the white car. I had no idea whether Dad was following me or not.

When we reached the lane, I heard him trotting behind me. I was glad. We needed to do this together.

"It's been great, Dad. We've had a brilliant time."

"Course we have. It was what I wanted—more than I hoped for. You're a great girl, Holly Starcross."

"You're not so bad yourself."

I kicked Rosa on, and we set off at a trot, then a canter, then a long, easy striding gallop that made my blood sing. Dad was beside me, and for the first time in my entire life I felt completely at ease with myself.

· 23 ·

Mum got out of the car as soon as we entered the yard. I'd planned to jump off Rosa and run to her and fling my arms around her. "I'm sorry I upset you," I'd planned to say, "but look what a wonderful time I've been having."

The look on her face froze me cold. She was not looking at me but at Dad, and her face was white with anger and something more, something worse. Dad jumped off Skipper and came toward her, holding out his hand, which she ignored. "Get in the car, Holly." Still not looking at me.

"You must be cold," Dad said. "The door was open. You could have gone in."

"You knew what time I was arriving. I've been sitting in this car for over an hour." Her voice was steady, but it wasn't calm. She flicked a glance at me. "Get in the car."

"Come in and have a cup of coffee," Dad said. "We need to talk things over."

"There's nothing to talk about. And I have no intention, ever, of going into that house again."

"I'd like to stay a bit longer—" I began, but Mum cut me short.

"And I'd like you to do as you're told. You've missed three days of school already. Get in."

I looked at Dad, and he jerked his head toward the car. I ran past him and up to my room, the room that I loved, with its deep window seat and the flickering, hushing sycamores outside, and the golden green hills. My beautiful room. Nana's cello. I changed out of Matty's old jeans and T-shirt and put my own clothes back on, the neat city girl clothes I'd been wearing when I came out of the library. I stuffed my books and the clothes Dad had bought me into my rucksack. I know I was crying, little soft, hiccuping bursts. I knew they were coming from me, and I couldn't control them. Outside I could hear Dad leading the horses into the stables. I could hear the thud of the saddles as he loosened them and slid them onto the ground. I could hear the dull throb of Mum's waiting engine.

I went downstairs. I had stopped crying. Mum was sitting in the car, tapping the steering wheel with the tips of her glossy painted fingernails. Dad came out of the stables and put his arms around me.

"I'll come back," I said. "I will."

I climbed into the car. Matty came out of the farmhouse next door and leaned on the gate. I raised my hand as we went past. He smiled and nodded and shut the gate behind us.

"I didn't say good-bye to Nana!"

Mum said nothing.

"Grandpa's very ill. Don't you care?"

"Have you any idea what I've been through in the last five days? Did *you* care?"

I couldn't say anything. I couldn't look back at Dad, or at the house. I couldn't look up at the hills with the sunlight pouring down them. I closed my eyes, and during the whole journey I didn't say a single word.

When we arrived, Zoe came crawling up the hallway, paddling along like a giant cat, laughing and turning her face up toward me. "Clever girl. You weren't doing that before! Clever, clever Zoe!"

I lifted her up, and she snuggled into my hair, straddling her legs around my waist and looping her arms around my neck. She smelled of baby powder and bananas.

Julian and Lisa ran out of the living room and stared at me.

"We thought you were dead," Lisa said.

"Course I wasn't dead. How could I possibly have been dead if I kept ringing you up?"

"We thought you were dead and somebody else was pretending to be you," said Julian.

"Why would anyone want to do that?"

He shrugged and ran back into the room to watch television. Lisa started crying. I know her. She was only putting it on, screwing her eyes shut as tight as she could as if she were squeezing juice out of lemons. Her face went red and blotchy and her breath shuddered.

"We . . . thought . . . you . . . were . . . dead. . . ."

Now, she can do this at any time. She can do it when

she doesn't want to go to bed or when she wants a chocolate biscuit, and Mum ignores her. But today Mum went and crouched down by her and put her arms around her. The trigger worked. Lisa collapsed into a sobbing heap.

"See!" Mum said. "See what you've done to us! We've been worried sick about you, all of us. We've not slept a wink."

Henry came out of the kitchen. He put his hands on my shoulders and said, "Welcome home. I've missed you." That was *my* trigger. I bundled Zoe into his arms and went upstairs to my room, my white sanctuary. Now I was home again, I was torn in half. I lay on my bed and howled like a baby. I howled out loud. I wanted them to hear me. I howled until I was exhausted. Panto padded into my room and jumped onto the bed, purr switched on full volume. I cuddled her like a baby.

Later, much later, when I was hung between sleeping and thinking, Henry came upstairs with a tray of food for me. He switched on the bedside light and arranged the pillows behind me as if I were a patient in a hospital, so I could sit up in bed and eat. I shifted food around my plate sulkily for a bit till real hunger got the better of me. Panto showed some interest in it, and I shoved her off the bed and ate everything on my plate.

Henry was jiggling about with the Internet on my computer while I was eating. He was looking up some information for a documentary he was making about diamonds. "Did you know," he said, "diamonds are made from graphite, same as pencils?"

I pushed away my empty plate, sighing. I didn't want

to compete with information. I didn't want to be told anything.

"You seemed to be the only ones who were glad to have me back," I said. "You and Zoe." I was in danger of howling again.

Henry closed down the computer and sat on the edge of my bed. "Don't believe it. You know your mother. She finds it very hard to express her feelings. She knew it was your father who had taken you away, and she wanted you back."

"To spite him."

"Listen to me. She went all that way on her own to collect you. She hates that house, but she went on her own for you."

"Why did she take me away from there in the first place?"

"Why? You *must* know why. Because she loved you, Holly."

· 24 ·

I went downstairs and phoned Dad. He sounded as if he was smiling, his voice as clear as if he were in the same room as I was. The little ones were asleep in bed. Henry was still upstairs asking the Internet how you could tell the difference between a fake diamond and a real one.

"How's Grandpa Jake?" I asked Dad.

"Missing his little Holly Heartthrob. We all are."

While I was on the phone, I was watching Mum reading a magazine. I wondered if she was listening to me talking to Dad. I hoped she was. I hoped it was hurting. I hung up, and she put down her magazine and patted the settee next to her, as if I were Panto or Zoe.

"Come and sit down," she said.

I didn't sit next to her but perched uncomfortably on the armchair opposite her. She picked up the TV control and switched on a soap. Someone was shouting at somebody else. They're always shouting at each other in soaps. So much aggro. The worst thing is when you're upstairs trying to do homework or something and there's all this energetic anger going on downstairs. Mum and Henry never shout, never.

"I've just phoned Dad," I said.

"I know."

"I want to go and see him again."

"No, Holly."

"You can't stop me."

"When you're eighteen you can do what you like."

"He could get a court order."

Her eyebrows flicked. "He won't."

Of course she was right. Dad had already told me that. It was a family matter. It was nothing to do with magistrates and courts. All I could understand was that it was to do with his relationship with Mum. She was stronger than he was. She would always get her own way. I knew that.

And then I found myself shouting, and it was like the television soap, only worse, much worse, because there were no words in the script for Mum. She just sat there wrapped in a cold and utter silence while I let out all my pain. I could have been with Dad all those years, I could have been in Low House, I could have been riding Rosa, playing Nana's cello, watching the birds in the sycamores. I told her all that, and I could hear my voice shouting words that could have been coming out of the television screen. And all the time Mum sat there as if she were made of ice. It was as if I could see right through her and there was nothing there, nothing at all.

Then she stood up and came over to me, slowly, awkwardly, like someone stiff from sitting for hundreds of years, like an ice creature stretching and melting. She bent down and put her arms around me. She sat on the arm of my chair. I knew that the ice had cracked and that she had heard me and she had listened to me.

The soap was coming to an end. She switched programs. "There's a documentary next," she said. "Wildlife. You like those, don't you?"

"Sometimes." My voice was still rusty with shouting. "I don't like it when the animals eat each other."

We both laughed. Mum, oh, Mum, I didn't mean to shout. Talk to me.

"I'll watch it with you," said Mum, who never watched programs about animals. "And when Henry stops playing on the Internet, we'll have a piece of chocolate cake."

I nodded. I was tired, too tired to watch television, too tired to wait up for Henry and eat chocolate cake, but I did all those things because my mum was sitting next to me with her arm around my shoulders.

Henry the hero did two things that week. He bought me a mobile so I could phone up my dad and talk to him anytime I wanted. And he suggested that Dad and Mum should meet up in a neutral place and talk. Mum was shocked at the idea, but somehow he reasoned and got her to listen. At first the suggestion was that they should meet alone, but I insisted that if they were going to talk about me, then I should be there, too.

"I know a good pub," I said, which made Henry smile and Mum shake her head in disbelief. "It's near where Dad left his car, and he'll have to go back there to collect it."

"What do you think?" Henry asked gently.

Mum shrugged. "I want you to come, too."

"Mum!" I protested.

"Henry has been your father for as long as that man has."

I stiffened at that, but I let it pass without saying anything. No one would replace my dad. Why couldn't she understand that? "We might as well take Julian and Lisa along." I tried to sound jokey. "And Zoe." I'd love Dad to see Zoe. When she heard her name, she chuckled and held out her hands to me. "Little Miss Sticky-fingers." I licked her fingers one by one, making her laugh out loud.

"Grandma will have them for the day," Henry said. "And I think you and Phil have a lot to say to each other that has nothing to do with me or Holly. I'll drive you there. I'd like to meet Phil. I'd like him to know that we're happy together. But then I'll go for a walk or something and come back for you."

Well, anything was better than nothing. I was going to see Dad again.

· 25 ·

I wore the clothes that Dad had bought for me. I could see by Mum's face that she didn't like them, but she said nothing. Henry brought Grandma Douglas around to look after the little ones.

"My, what a Worzel Gummidge you look!" She laughed.

She comes out with these things. I haven't a clue what she's on about half the time.

"She looks very nice," Henry said. He wasn't even looking at me, but I appreciated the effort.

Grandma hugged me and whispered to me that I mustn't do anything to hurt my mum. "She was like a fish out of water in that place. Don't blame her for any of this."

Who was to blame then? Me? For being six years old and dependent at the time? No, I wasn't blaming anyone. I was past all that. What good did it do? I kissed

Grandma, I don't know why. I was excited about seeing Dad again.

In the car Henry asked me a lot about Rosa and the other ponies and about Nana Zosia and the cello. Mum was listening intently, pretending to be absorbed in the traffic. The overwhelming scent of her perfume dried my nostrils and pricked my eyes and my skin. Why was she wearing so much? I could taste it. I couldn't get away from it, even when I wound down the window of the car. She wore it as if it were part of her, like her gleaming hair or her glossy nails. At times I wondered whether I liked her at all, and then I thrust the thought away, ashamed. Of course I liked her. She was my mother.

I told Henry about my lovely room facing the hills, and the cherry tree that the tawny owl roosted in, and the sycamores. I didn't tell him about Matty, how his hair slipped across his left eye like a pirate's patch, how he grinned at me in the yard. He was a secret. I didn't know till then that I wanted him to be a secret.

Dad's battered old car was in the pub car park, and he was crouched on his haunches, deep in conversation with a spaniel that was tied up to a tree. When he saw us, he straightened up and waved, smiling. He was wearing the old multicolored sweater that he loved so much. For a second I wished that he had smartened himself up for Mum's sake, but then I realized that it wasn't his way, any more than Mum could have worn a simple pair of jeans and a sweater for him. She was wearing the sort of clothes that she would wear on her program: a pale green suit that showed off the gold of her hair, the jade earrings that I loved, which hid and winked in the swing of her hair. Her high heels made her taller than he was. She looked beautiful. She always does. People always look at Mum. And she looked very calm. Henry squeezed her hand and whispered something in her ear. It sounded like "I love you." It probably was.

She climbed out of the car and smiled her stunning smile. I scrambled out and ran to Dad and flung my arms around him, and he hugged me like a great woolly bear. He smelled of horses. When we turned around, Henry was standing next to Mum. They looked terrific together, blond and blue-eyed. Henry in his immaculate, expensive suit and light blue polo-necked sweater. He held out his hand to Dad.

"This is Henry," I said.

Dad clasped his hand warmly. "It's good to meet you, Henry. Holly's told me a lot about you."

"You, too, Phil."

I could hear this chanting in my head as if I were a fairy waving a wand to cast a spell on them. Like each other. Like each other. Be friends.

Henry touched Mum's arm. "Give me a call when you're ready. I won't be far away."

I saw, for a moment, a flicker of panic in Mum's eyes as he got back into the car. Then she regained her composure, and her lovely public smile came back. I felt how fragile she was. Suddenly I wanted to protect her. I linked my arm into hers. "They do lovely cappuccinos here." How I would have loved to have linked my other arm in Dad's.

There was a big log fire burning in the pub. I could

see how the flames mesmerized Mum, just like the screen saver on my computer. "What do you see in them?" Dad asked gently. She looked startled for a moment as if it were an intimate question, digging into her daydreams.

"It's just the way the patterns keep changing. There's nothing still. It's like watching the sea, only better."

"And outside your safe cave the woolly mammoths and the bears are prowling under the huge stars."

I went quietly to the bar and ordered three cappuccinos. I was quivering with hope. They were getting on. They liked each other. I heard Mum laugh, and I turned and looked at her. Her face was lit by the flames; her hair gleamed. Surely Dad would fall in love with her. And he looked so happy, so relaxed. How could she hate him now?

"Where are you sitting?" the barman asked, unnecessarily, I thought, as there were only three other people in the whole place.

"By the fire." Equally unnecessarily, I added, "With my mum and dad." There was a flutter of pride in my voice. I heard it.

I wandered back to them. Dad was reminding Mum about a bonfire party in the village when all the children had made a wicker man for a guy.

"I remember it!" She laughed. "It was enormous. They all processed down the village with him to the playing fields. Holly was holding his hand! She was only five. I was so upset for them all. They'd spent days making him, and now they were taking him to be burned! I thought they'd be inconsolable."

"And did we cry?"

Mum looked at me, puzzled. I think she'd forgotten that I was there.

"No. As soon as the fire was lit, you all started cheering and shouting, and you thought it was wonderful! Wonderful! I just couldn't understand it."

I tried to think of the wicker man sinking into flames, and all I could see was the ice man shouldering himself into sunlight. I would tell Zed about this. *Zed!*

The cappuccinos arrived. I scooped up my froth with my spoon. Dad laughed. "Now that reminds me of Grandpa Jake. That time we took him out for a birthday meal and afterward we ordered cappuccinos. He wouldn't have that, of course, probably because he couldn't pronounce it. He ordered tea."

Mum laughed. "And when the cappuccinos came, Holly ate the froth with her spoon, just the way she's doing now."

"And poor old Dad obviously thought that's what you had to do when you ate out posh, and he dipped his spoon in his cup of tea as if it was a bowl of soup and drank it down."

We all laughed, gales of laughter. I was crying with laughing. The other people in the pub turned around to stare at us. What a happy family party we must have looked. I loved my mum and dad. I loved them both. It was all right to love them both.

"How is the old chap these days?"

"Dying," Dad said, and I looked at him quickly with my laughing caught back like a sob. Grandpa Jake, striding over the hills to see his young sweetheart. Searching the world for his little dark-eyed Zosia. Old man. Dying.

The laughing had gone, and it never came again.

"How's your father?" Dad asked.

"He died," Mum said. "A couple of years ago."

"I'm sorry. I liked Bill."

"He never liked you." Mum stared at her coffee, the froth gone flat, the chocolate powder smeared down the side of the cup.

We were silent. It wasn't a comfortable silence. There were things to be said—that was why we had come—and now was the time to say them. A woman in a flow-ered head scarf put some money in the flashing fruit machine, and it juddered around, apples, cherries, pineapples. Her husband sat in a cloud of blue smoke. "Give it a kick," he advised.

"I'm pleased you came," Dad said quietly.

The bandit player scored. Coins jetted out noisily. "Thank you, my darling," the woman crooned, scoop-ing up her winnings. "Lucky Lily, that's me."

"About Holly," Dad said.

"Yes, about Holly."

About me. About me.

Dad smiled at me. It's going to be all right, his eyes said. "This seems to be a good halfway place. If you don't want her to travel on her own yet, you could bring her this far, and she could come on with me."

"What are you talking about?" Mum's voice was cold and sharp and strained. Her cheekbones showed white through her makeup.

"Every couple of weeks or so. You could bring Holly here, we could have a coffee and a bit of a chat, and she could come home with me for the weekend." He was still smiling, but he wasn't looking at me anymore, and he wasn't relaxed.

"It's a three-hour drive. It's out of the question."

"Mum, don't say no. You can't say no." I could already feel the chill of her ice around her.

"I am saying no. It's always been out of the question. I'm not prepared to put my child through this . . . this kind of dislocation. The carrier bag kid, being passed backward and forward every week like a piece of luggage. It's out of the question."

"It's not as simple as that." Dad's voice was very level and quiet, but I could tell he was trying to control himself. I bet he wanted to shake her. I know I did. She was so calm, so sure of herself. "She's my daughter, too. There are two of us to consider here."

"Three of us!" I could hardly bear it. "You haven't asked me what *I* want."

The barman came over and wiped the table where I'd spilled some froth. "Did you want anything else?"

"No," said Mum.

"Thank you," said Dad.

The head-scarf woman fed the machine again. The flashing fruit rolled around.

"Holly is right," Mum said. "She's the one who has to be considered. I think we should ask her to choose."

"What?" I stared at her. You know what I want. Surely you know what I want. I want you both.

And Mum, who must have read my frightened, unspoken thoughts, said, "You can't have us both. It won't work. You have to choose."

"Diane!" Dad protested, and was cut short.

"Now. I want you to choose now. You can choose which of us you want to live with, which of us you want to go home with. And we must abide by it. It's the only way. Choose, Holly. Choose now. What do you want?"

No, her voice wasn't calm. It was breaking into tiny pieces, like a wall of stone crumbling into pebbles. Her eyes were glistening. I couldn't look at her anymore. I couldn't look at Dad. I could hear him breathing slowly and heavily. I watched his hands spreading out in a strange, hopeless gesture and then coming together on the table, clasping together, knuckles white. I felt as if the room were opening and closing around me, as if the room were breathing, as if it were taking deep, listening, waiting breaths. The people in the room, the flames in the fire, the bright lights and reflections had all broken up into tiny crystal motes of color and were spiraling slowly around me. I couldn't speak. I couldn't think. I put my head in my hands and closed everything away from me. I saw Zoe's laughing face. I saw Rosa in her sweet-smelling stable. I saw my rose-colored room and the pattern of cherry tree leaves flickering on the walls. I saw my white modern room with its shelves of CDs and the computer flashing on my desk. I saw Sandy waving to me from the top of the bus. Nana Zosia, her busy, bright eyes, her cello—*my* cello, its hard, satiny body and its honey golden voice. Aaron Hamilton. I saw Matty leaning on the farm gate, mud on his boots, holes in his sweater. Dad, comfortable and easy, poking the kitchen fire to get some heat in the house. Mum, beautiful and smiling. Her golden family. Grandpa Jake.

When I opened my eyes at last, a million years later, I

172 •

didn't know where I was. I had been in a deep sleep of enchantment. Everything was as it had been before, moving again and breathing, the fire was dancing, the barman was whistling and wiping glasses, the head-scarf woman was feeding coins into the machine, Mum was sitting elegant and still. But Dad—my dad had gone.

· 26 ·

I ran out into the car park. Dad's car was just pulling out into the main road. "Dad!" I yelled. "Dad, don't go!"

He didn't hear me. If he did, he took no notice.

I went blindly back into the pub. Mum was paying the barman for the coffees. She smiled at me. "Typical of a man," she joked. "To leave without paying."

The barman shrugged and turned up the music. It was a really bad country and western song, the sort that makes your toes curl with embarrassment. Mum hummed to it while she fumbled in her bag. She found her mobile and rang Henry. "Yes, we're both here. Yes, we're fine."

She put the phone away, very slowly, very carefully thinking through what she was going to say next. "You see, Holly, that is exactly what I would expect of your father."

I knew she wasn't talking about the bill for the coffees.

"Of course he loves you. There's no denying that. But when it comes to the *crunch*, when he's faced with the possibility of having you all the time, all the responsibility and expense that implies, he couldn't handle it. It would change his life. He's a man who's set in his ways, as I found out when I lived with him. It's for the best. He sees that as well as I do. *We're* your family. You have a lovely home. A good school. Lots of friends. What does he have to offer? He can't expect you to give all that up and go and live in that place with him."

Okay, Mum. Okay. Leave me alone. I've had enough.

She put her arm through mine, leading me to a chair as if I were suddenly infirm. "He could have traced you years ago if he'd really wanted to. There are ways of doing it. But it didn't suit him then, and it doesn't suit him now. Oh, he had some kind of romantic fantasy about seeing his little girl again. But you're not a little girl anymore. He's a romantic. He's a storyteller. He hasn't got a practical bone in his body, except when it comes to looking after horses." She laughed scornfully.

"Don't you like him at all?" I didn't want her to talk like this. Dad was slipping away into my dreams again; she was pushing him there.

"Like? He's a very likable man. But love is a different matter, if that's what you're talking about."

"Then why did you marry him?"

"Henry said he'll be about ten minutes. Do you want another coffee?"

I shook my head. Why didn't she answer me, ever? Why did she never answer my questions? Dad was like an open book when he talked to me. Mum made me feel like a prying infant.

"Let's wait outside then. I can't stand that man's pipe smoke."

I followed her out. It was warmer now, in the middle of the day. We sat on one of the garden benches. I was watching the drift of golden leaves, like a dream, like an enchantment.

Mum said, "You asked me why I married your father."

I froze, listening intently, not watching her at all.

"Something you don't know, Holly, is that I was married at eighteen."

"How old was Dad?"

"No, not to your dad. A man called Max. He was going to get me into films; he was going to take me to Hollywood; he was going to make me into a star. He turned my head completely. I believed him. We went to America. Oh, yes, he had all the right connections. I met loads of people who flattered me and told me I could act, which I couldn't, or that I didn't need to act, just look gorgeous. It was terribly exciting. But predictably Max left me for a rising Italian beauty. Dumped me, as you say today. I didn't get a part in a film. Luckily, I didn't get pregnant either. But I was still being courted, and I was still in the media circle. I had lots of boyfriends after Max. One was a documentary producer called Doug. But I was beginning to be tired of all that glamour.

"Doug was making a documentary up in Derbyshire. Something to do with horses. I needed a break from

London. I came up for a holiday. Doug introduced me to a horse trainer he was interviewing."

My heart jumped. "That was Dad."

"Exactly. And he was so different from all those other men. For a start, he didn't even see me! All he saw was horses! And he had a lovely sense of humor. I liked him a lot. It was such a change to be treated like a normal person! He told me about Low House, and it sounded like heaven to me. I had to get away, from Doug, from everything. Phil offered me peace and quiet away from the public eye, and I thought it would be the most wonderful thing in the world. He was very correct. We had to be married. A quiet wedding in the village. He did love me. And for a time I loved him. You were born a year later."

Ghostly. I had shivers all down my spine while she was talking. This is real, Mum.

"And then, simply, I stopped loving him."

Before Sandy, my best friend was Rebecca Holloway. I met her as soon as I started at junior school, and we were inseparable. We walked around with our arms around each other's waists. She came on holiday with us to our French house. I went with her raucous, gum-chewing family to Brighton, and at night we shared a bed and whispered secrets to each other. We spent hours doing each other's hair. I wouldn't have a word said against her, even though Mum really disliked her. I was sick with jealousy if I thought anyone was trying to come between us. And then one day we fell out. She was furious because I'd accepted an invitation to a birthday party that she hadn't been invited to. I looked at her red, scowling, gum-chewing face and I thought, I don't like you. "I don't want to be friends with you anymore," I said, and I ran home crying because I knew I meant it. I thought about those glorious years of secrets and whispers and giggles, and I knew that it was true. It was over. I couldn't stand her anymore. I watched her in the playground and wondered what I had seen in her.

Is it like that, anything like that, with grown-ups who were in love and then stop loving each other? Do they hate each other then? Is that what it was like for Mum and my father?

The white car pulled into the forecourt. Henry leaned out, smiling, and blew Mum a kiss. If he'd been anxious about her seeing Dad, he didn't show it for a moment. I realized that they were absolutely confident with each other, absolutely at ease. In love. Even I could see that. Maybe after all those mistakes Mum had really found the right person for her. I suppose I should feel happy about that.

"In you get," Mum said. And before I did, she squeezed my hand.

Henry and Mum chatted as if nothing had happened. I sat in the back thinking about everything she had told me. She had never talked to me like that before. She was kind of trusting me. And I thought about Dad, driving away without saying a word to me.

Oh, Dad, how could you have done that to me? After all this?

Grandma Douglas had made a cake while we were out. She always does. The house smelled wonderful. Lisa and

Julian were being model children, helping her in the kitchen. They had made little sponge cakes and put them on the best plate, so we had to eat them as soon as we went in, with Lisa watching solemnly for our reaction.

"I'll take mine upstairs," I said. "I don't want it at the moment."

And Mum slammed around to me, and I knew that nothing had changed, nothing. "You will not take it upstairs," she said. "Stop hiding up there. You are part of this family, Holly Murray."

"Holly Starcross," said Julian, "that's what she calls herself." Important with the information, knowing nothing of its significance. "I'm going to be Julian Cake-maker."

"I'm Lisa Sticky-bun." Lisa giggled. They romped around the kitchen, rolling cakes at each other across the table, brats again.

"May I remind you that you promised to be on your best behavior," said Grandma helplessly.

"We are." Lisa giggled, red-faced and spluttering crumbs. "This *is* our best behavior."

And I was forgotten. Wearily I climbed the stairs.

Why did you go, Dad? Why didn't you even say good-bye? What do I do now?

You've left me adrift without a compass.

I switched on the computer. Message from Sandy. **What happened? Tell me you're not going to move. I can't bear the thought of it.**

I typed back. **Nothing happened. I'm still here. It seems Dad didn't want me after all.**

I switched off the computer, lay on my bed. Hours. Put on some music. Switched it off again. Went to sleep.

Woke up. Julian and Lisa going to bed, stamping up the stairs. Put my computer back on. Logged on to my e-mail. Message from Zed.

Do not expect the one who loves you most to pull you in half.

· 27 ·

Of course! Of course! Of course!

I fished my new mobile out of my schoolbag. A few seconds later I was talking to Dad. I was happier than I'd ever been in my life.

I ran downstairs, singing. Mum and Grandma Douglas were in the kitchen, stacking up the dishwasher after the meal that I had missed.

"Here comes my favorite grandchild," Grandma said. "Do you know, you're a different girl when you smile?"

"I knew she'd come round," Mum said.

"You go and sit down," I told Grandma. "I'll help Mum."

I felt very relaxed with Mum now. I was reeling through things in my head, all those stories that Dad had told me, all those chapters of my family story. But there was still one chapter missing.

"Mum."

She turned around, absorbed in counting out the cutlery that went in the boxed canteen. When she frowned like that, she looked older. I put my arms around her, and surprised, she put her arms around me. She had a handful of spoons. I could feel their sharp edges digging into my back. She kissed the top of my head. "Fuzzy mop!" she said. "What do you want?"

The end of the story. "Why did you take me away from Dad?"

She pulled herself away from me, with her arms still stretched onto my shoulders. "Oh, Holly! Surely you know why?"

I took the spoons out of her hand. I loved putting the silver into its box. It was like a family, and each had a place. The big serving spoons were the grandparents. The knives and forks were the father and mother. The soup spoons and dessert spoons were the aunties and uncles, and the little knives and forks were the children. The lovely shiny teaspoons were the babies. Zoe the teaspoon. While I was thinking all this and finding their places, I was saying the most difficult thing I had ever said to anyone.

"Was it my fault?"

"What?"

"That day—I wanted to go with Daddy to Vincent's farm. I loved going with him. When you said I couldn't go, I kept crying and shouting. I was horrible. I kept shouting that I wanted to be with my daddy. I cried myself to sleep, wanting to be with him. And when I woke up, Henry was there, and you took me away." I turned to look at Mum. "Was that why you took me with you?"

She sat down on the stool. Her face had sagged. "Is this what you've been thinking all these years?"

"Yes."

"Holly, it wasn't your fault. None of it was your fault. I had no intention of leaving your father without taking you with me. I wasn't planning to leave you behind."

"But was it because I used to want to be with him all the time?" So difficult. So hard to say, so hard to answer. But nothing will stop me now. I'm like a dog, digging holes to look for bones. No, I'm an ice girl, rising out of her hiding place as the sun pours down on her frozen limbs and warms her to life, as the crystals drop away from her. See me, Mum. The sun's shining on me. I'm happy.

"I suppose it was."

"And was that why you wouldn't let me see him or write to him?"

"It's more complicated than that. It was nothing to do with you. I never wanted to see him again."

"You seemed to get on all right with him the other day."

She looked at me as if I were speaking a foreign language, puzzled, reading my lips, reading my eyes. "You're not even fifteen yet. How can you hope to understand?" She stood up and closed the lid of the cutlery canteen, tidying it away, tidying up our talk.

And I went upstairs and tidied my room. I sorted through all my books and CDs and videos. Some of them I put in a bag for Oxfam. They belonged to a child who used to be me. I did the same with my clothes. I packed the things I wanted into my rucksack, and then I ran downstairs and lifted Panto off the settee and put her into the cat basket. Grandma had fallen asleep with her mouth open. I put the cat basket and my rucksack in the hall. I went into the room that Lisa and Julian shared. Henry was telling them a story. Lisa was already asleep with her thumb in her mouth. Julian's eyes kept flickering shut. I wondered how many unfinished stories they had in their heads.

I went into Mum and Henry's room. Mum's clothes were lying across the bed. She was in the bathroom having a shower before work; she and Henry had a late-night recording session to do. Zoe was asleep in her cot. I lifted her out, and she stirred drowsily, warm and sweet-smelling.

"I don't know how I can bear to leave you," I told her.

She yawned, pushing her fists into her eyes, and began to whimper. Mum came out of her bathroom wearing a pale blue silk dressing gown. Her hair was loose. She looked about sixteen again.

"What have you woken her up for?" she grumbled. "I'll never get her off again now, and Mother doesn't like having to get her to sleep."

I lowered Zoe back into the cot. "I was saying goodbye to her," I said.

"What do you mean?"

I took a deep breath. I levered my arm away from Zoe's grasp and said the second most difficult thing I had ever said in my life. "I'm going to live with Dad."

I could have gone without saying anything. Before Mum and Henry came back from the television studios, Dad would have arrived. I could have just left a note. I could have done what she had done and just walked out. I could have bundled Zoe up and taken her with me. I could have done any of those things, and I would have been running away. But I wasn't running away.

"I'll be back at Christmas," I told her. "And at Easter."

"What about your schoolwork?" she asked weakly. As if she had ever worried about my schoolwork before.

"They have schools in Derbyshire, you know."

She stared at me, and she couldn't think of anything else to say, and neither could I.

I left her to get herself dressed and ready. She would probably do some yoga to calm herself down. I heard Henry having a shower. He was whistling cheerfully, and she said something to him, and he stopped whistling, and I knew she'd told him. The phone rang, and she answered it. It was Dad, already on his way, wanting to know if I had told her. I heard her voice, raised and sharp, and then leveling out. Calm and steady. Calm and steady.

Henry came up to my room. "Are you sure this is what you want?"

"Yes. Quite, quite sure. Eight years' worth of sure." I just couldn't stop smiling. My cheeks hurt with smiling. "Nobody's going to make me change my mind."

"I can see that." He put his hand on my shoulder, awkward, a bit rueful.

When they were ready to go to the studio, I came out

of my room and hugged them both. "No need to cry," I said to Mum. "Watch your mascara." She even managed a weak smile. I hugged her again, and this time I meant it; I really meant it.

Grandma Douglas woke up and came out of the living room. They stood in a row staring at me and then at my rucksack and at the cat basket with Panto fast asleep in it, waiting by the front door for Dad to come. Funny, I felt more grown-up than any of them. They didn't know what to *do*. I did. I was going home.

And then, wowee! Mum and Henry went to work.

"You *are* a different girl," Grandma said. "You're growing up fast. Do you know, I'm proud of you, Holly Starcross."

I ran up to my room and put my music on, really loud, and jumped onto my bed. I bounced up and down on it, higher and higher, singing at the top of my voice.

I tell you, if my roof window had been open, I'd have bounced right out of it. I'd have hit my head on the stars.